COMMENDATIONS

Wes Richards has been a wonderful friend to us over many years. His first book, **Hope and a Future**, was a profound story of loss and how the providential hand of God guided him through a desperately challenging time. Now Wes and Adriana have written of their own journey of finding unexpected romance and later-life cross-cultural love, once more in a deeply personal and often humorous style, which will touch hearts both inside and outside of the church.

NICKY AND PIPPA GUMBEL,
PIONEERS OF THE GLOBAL ALPHA COURSE AND AUTHORS OF THE BIBLE IN ONE YEAR

Pastor Wes Richards has been a faithful shepherd, at King's Church International and through his global ministry for over 40 years. His first book, **Hope and A Future**, about how God sustained him and his family with hope and healing after losing his dear wife to cancer, is now followed with this uplifting sequel. It's the story of how the Lord brought Wes and his lovely Colombian bride Adriana together in an extraordinary way. Read it! It will encourage you.

DR RT KENDALL, INTERNATIONAL SPEAKER AND AUTHOR

God is an expert in love and can surprise us in the most unexpected moments. In this story two cultures, two languages, and two very different worlds come together for a greater purpose. Wes and Adriana are a couple full of lessons; their lives inspire us and show us, through their example, how God's love can surprise us in incredible ways. On every page of this book, God will speak to your heart.

ELIEMERSON AND JOHANNA PROENÇA CASTELLANOS, OVERSEEING PASTORS OF A LARGE NETWORK OF CHURCHES IN COLOMBIA AND BRAZIL

The first time we met Wes and Adriana together, we were truly amazed at how two gifted individuals were hardly able to communicate together in the same language. Yet we could not miss the spark of love in their eyes. Their cultural and language differences did not stop the love that grew between them proving that true love knows no boundaries. Their shared faith is the strong and steady foundation upon which they have built their marriage.

BARRY AND BATYA SEGAL, CO-FOUNDERS OF THE JOSEPH STOREHOUSE, A HUMANITARIAN CHARITY

SURPRISED BY LOVE

FINDING TRUE LOVE WHEN YOU LEAST EXPECT IT

WES & ADRIANA RICHARDS

FOREWORD BY
CÉSAR & EMMA CLAUDIA CASTELLANOS

WESRICHARDS.CO.UK

Copyright © 2024 by Wes and Adriana Richards

This edition copyright © 2024

The right of Wes and Adriana Richards to be identified as authors of this work has been asserted by them in accordance with the Copyright, Designs and Patent Act 1988.

All rights reserved. No part of this publication may be reproduced or transmitted in any form or by any means, electronic or mechanical, including photocopy, recording or any information storage and retrieval system, without permission in writing from the authors, except for the use of brief quotations.

ISBN: 9798300920227

First edition 2024

Acknowledgements

Scripture quotations taken from Holy Bible, New International Version® Anglicized, NIV® Copyright © 1979, 1984, 2011 by Biblica, Inc.® Used by permission. All rights reserved worldwide.

Scripture quotations marked MSG are taken from *THE MESSAGE*, copyright © 1993, 2002, 2018 by Eugene H. Peterson. Used by permission of NavPress. All rights reserved. Represented by Tyndale House Publishers, Inc.

A catalogue record for this book is available from the British Library.

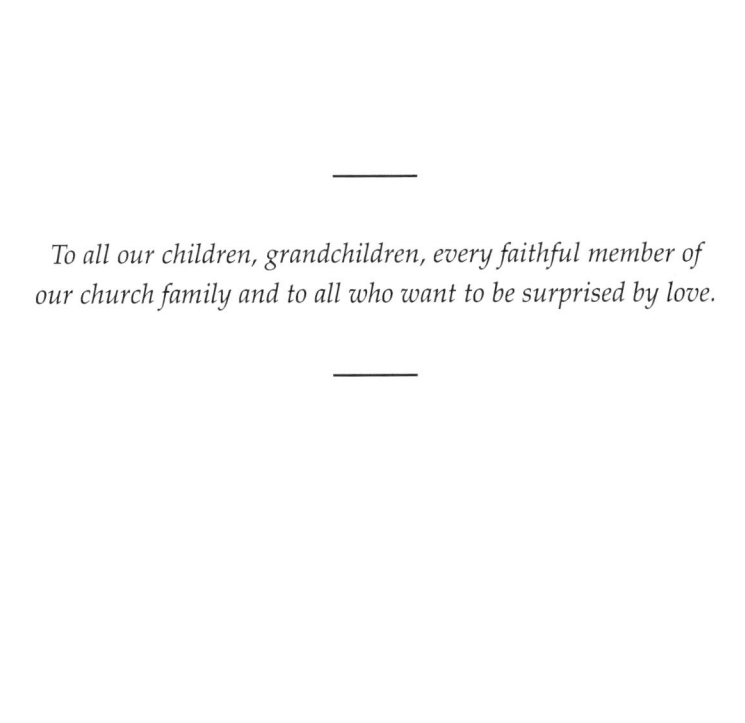

To all our children, grandchildren, every faithful member of our church family and to all who want to be surprised by love.

ABOUT THE AUTHORS

Wes Richards is the senior pastor of King's Church International in Windsor and London, UK and in Robertson, South Africa. The church was started in Slough with just five people in 1943 by Wes's father, Pastor Billy Richards, a former Welsh coalminer.

A former London evening newspaper journalist and feature writer, Pastor Wes has spoken at many large national and international events including Spring Harvest, New Frontiers International, and the annual international G12 conferences where he has addressed two presidents. He is also the UK coordinator for the G12 International movement.

Pastor Wes holds a master's degree in theology which featured a dissertation on the spiritual, social, economic, and political impact of the global Holy Spirit movement.

In 2012, Pastor Wes founded The King's House School Windsor, a Christian school for 3–13-year-olds, which offers an education incorporating academic excellence, an affirming Christian community, character development, and the teaching of a Bible based worldview.

Today, Pastor Wes has thirteen grandchildren, two step grandchildren, three married children, their spouses, three stepchildren and their spouses following his wedding in Miami in 2016 to his second wife, Adriana Richards from Bogotá, Colombia.

Adriana Richards shares the senior pastors' responsibilities of King's Church International alongside her husband.

A successful businesswoman, Pastor Adriana has a degree in business administration and a master's degree in marketing. She ran an award-winning insurance agency for many years.

Pastor Adriana became a Christian at MCI church in Bogotá, where she was involved in leadership roles.

She and Pastor Wes have spoken at many large national and international events in Europe, Africa, Asia, and North and South America. She also hosts a popular annual women's conference in the UK.

Her three children and two granddaughters now live close to her in the UK, and she regularly co-hosts family gatherings with her husband for all her and Pastor Wes's blended family. She is also a gifted interior and garden designer.

instagram.com/wesrichards12

youtube.com/@wesandadrianarichards5637

FOREWORD

Surprised by Love would make a great movie. For it is not just the fascinating story of the marriage between a romantic Englishman and a beautiful Colombian woman. It is also the testimony of how two people from different continents, who didn't speak the same language, continued to believe in the possibility of being surprised by love, even at a stage in their lives when many would have given up on that dream.

Though they both had experienced pain and loss, they did not remain in their sadness but allowed themselves to be healed and restored. Instead of closing themselves off to love, they asked God to guide them and to open new paths to a union that has already inspired thousands.

Their shared dedication and commitment have borne fruit both in their growing families and in their leadership of a multicultural church, which has become a refuge for people of diverse nations and cultures.

Today, their marriage is a living example of how God can restore and bring hope even in the most challenging times. In these pages, you will find not only the story of an unusual marriage, but also faith and inspiration.

César & Emma Claudia Castellanos
Founders of one of the world's largest churches in Bogotá, Colombia

CONTENTS

Introduction	xv
Prologue	1
1. Adriana's Story: Learning to Dream Again	5
2. Adriana's Story: The Long Wait for Love	17
3. Wes's Story: Slowly Waking Up to New Possibilities	29
4. Meeting Up at Last	41
5. And Now it Begins	53
6. Taking the Plunge	65
7. Meeting up in Miami	77
8. Lady in the Dream	89
9. Engaged in Cartagena	101
10. O Happy Day	113
11. A Very Different Kind of Honeymoon	125
12. Long Hot Summer of Love	137
13. A Year of Jubilee	149
14. Living Happily Ever After	159
From Us to You, with Love	173
A Prayer for New Beginnings	177
Acknowledgments	179
Legal Acknowledgements	181
About Hope And A Future	183
For More Information	185

INTRODUCTION

You can find true love even when you least expect it. You never know when a whole new world can open for you. Whether you are younger or older, you can still live the best dream.

Maybe you have been battered by many storms in life, but your life does not need to end up on the rocks. It's not too late for you to find love.

You can still find hope and a future. This was the theme of my first book after my family and I discovered how we could live again after a great loss. I wrote: *"Just because you are down, it doesn't mean you are out. You may think your life is finished. But the reality may very well be that a life you never imagined is only just beginning."*

Well, as events turned out, a new beginning that I certainly never imagined awaited me personally. And that's why I have written this sequel to the first book. For, after nearly 14 years as a widower and with 13 grandkids to keep me busy, out of nowhere my life changed suddenly and dramatically.

The great author C.S. Lewis wrote that he was *Surprised by Joy*. I also have been surprised by joy but especially by love... a love that has overcome some very big differences between languages, cultures and continents.

If you read on, as we invite you to, I promise you that the Anglo/Hispanic story that my beautiful Colombian wife and I tell is going to sound much more far-fetched than a fairy tale. You really couldn't make it up. But it's all very real, "autentico" as they say in Spanish, and we have had a lot of fun and fulfilment along the way.

Our story shows how you too can find new and unexpected favour in your life.

INTRODUCTION

Our first picture together in Bogotá, 2016.

PROLOGUE

El Campín Coliseum, Bogotá, Colombia, late January 2008

Colombia is a land of surprises. It is one of the most beautiful countries in the world and its people, despite its troubled history, are typically warm and welcoming.

I had witnessed the many positive changes in the country's safety and prosperity since my first visit in 2003.

But now, five years later, as I arrived at the newly renovated El Dorado International Airport in Bogotá, I received some news that caught me off guard. Our guide casually informed me that I was to be the first speaker the next day at a conference attended by 18,000 delegates from around the world. Obviously, something somewhere had been lost in translation for I had not come prepared to speak at a gathering considerably larger than any that I had previously addressed.

The next morning, after having had a good night's rest and spending time in earnest prayer, I was getting ready to walk up from the basement of the multi-level El Campín Coliseum, next to the national El Campín football stadium.

As my name was loudly announced, I pictured the actor Russell Crowe as he entered the noisy arena in the film *Gladiator*. Fortunately, it was not lions who awaited me but a great crowd of very animated Christians. It was like walking into a furnace of energy. There was a buzz of anticipation similar to a kick-off at a big match.

It was quite a sight with so many people and so many colourful national flags and banners all over the place. It could have all been increasingly intimidating as I approached the very small podium at the front and centre of a very large platform. Yet, as I began to speak, I felt very calm and, strangely, very much at home.

At the last moment I had decided to leave my carefully prepared notes and quotes backstage and just speak from my heart. I wanted to simply tell the story of how I, and our close-knit family, had experienced an unexpected new beginning following the death, from cancer, of Carol, my teenage sweetheart and wife of 29 years.

I shared how I had asked God to somehow help me recover from a deep grief that had felt like it would overwhelm me and, especially, how I had prayed that our three children, Wesley, James, and Melody, would find healing and hope. I related how 18 months after I had prayed, James and Wesley had married two sisters from South Africa in separate ceremonies on one weekend.

This was followed two years later by the marriage of my daughter, Melody, to the brother of the two sisters.

At this news there was widespread laughter but also, I could see that many people were moist-eyed. I, too, was moved in recounting the story. I was also touched to see my two sons and their wives out in the crowd, now each holding their first-born sons.

In a freeze-frame moment, I thought I had captured a perfect picture of how God had been faithful to answer my prayers for our broken family. I marvelled at how far we had come on a journey of recovery and restoration. But, as I was to learn several years later, I was only seeing part of a much bigger picture.

What I didn't know at that time was that, as I spoke, the seeds of a new future for my own life were being sown. For way up in the vertigo-inducing seats just under the roof, was a first-time visitor, a beautiful Colombian lady who had experienced considerable sadness in her own life. She was listening to our family story with great interest. Her name, I discovered years later, was Adriana Bastidas Rodriquez.

On that remarkable day in Bogotá's Coliseum, now known as the Movistar Arena, neither she nor I could have ever imagined how the very different stories of our lives would one day come together.

CHAPTER 1
ADRIANA'S STORY: LEARNING TO DREAM AGAIN

I hadn't really known what to expect when a friend invited me to a big event at one of Bogotá's most famous venues. I had been to many business, political and sporting gatherings over the years but this was to be my first visit to an international Christian conference.

As we concentrated on carefully climbing high up to our seats, I had no idea that I was also stepping into a whole new world of future possibilities. Nor did I imagine how much I was about to be inspired to have faith for new beginnings in my life after experiencing so much heartache and disillusionment. And I certainly didn't expect to start dreaming again about romance. In truth, I had many broken dreams.

My life began happily enough when I was born in one of the most beautiful locations in the world: Cali, Colombia. The temperatures are always around 30 degrees Celsius, cooled by afternoon breezes from the two surrounding Andes Mountain ranges and the Pacific coast. Its people are relaxed and friendly and are famous for their love of up-tempo music and Salsa dancing.

In my early years, before it became a notorious centre of drug cartels, Cali was an idyllic place to grow up. I felt very loved and secure. When I was four, however, my perfect world was suddenly shattered. My Mum and Dad, whom I both loved very much, got divorced. I was very sad and found everything very confusing.

When our parents split, my younger brother, Carlos, and I moved with our Mum to live with her parents. My Dad moved to another part of the city, and we rarely saw him. I missed him terribly.

Once, when I was seven, I ran away to try and meet him. I had saved some pocket money to pay the fare for a bus that would take me near where he worked. It was quite a long journey, but I got off at the right stop and found him. I was overjoyed to see him. He was shocked to see me and couldn't believe that I had travelled so far on my own. He gave me a lot of hugs and some presents, bread, and cakes, before returning me home to my very worried family. I had to promise everyone to never do that again.

For a while, my mum took my brother and I to visit him but my dad moved to another city and from then on we lost contact. I didn't see him again for 35 years. I always wondered what became of him and whether or not he still loved us.

A few years later, my mother got married again to a man from Venezuela and decided to relocate to live with him there. She wanted to take us with them, but my grandparents and aunties insisted that we should not be uprooted from the very close family network in Cali. So, they ended up looking after us. My Mum visited three or four times a year and was generous in sending us money to help us.

Despite greatly missing my parents, I have many happy memories of my childhood. I enjoyed getting up early and helping at my grandad's neighbourhood bakery. He was very popular and seemed to know everyone. To this day, I love the smell of freshly made bread.

My Grandmother was kind and a devout Roman Catholic. She took me to Mass every day and would insist that we knelt down to pray beside our beds each night before we went to sleep. Sometimes she prayed so long that I had no problem sleeping.

I remember thinking many times that my grandmother was too strict, but, in hindsight, I can see that she encouraged me to have faith in God. Even though I didn't have any personal experience with God, I still heard about His love. I remember how happy I felt when I took my first communion at nine years of age.

My grandfather, on the other hand, was not as committed to the church, but they both agreed to send us to a school taught by nuns. Sometimes I got into trouble for joking, but despite my mischievous behaviour, I mostly got on well with the nuns. I even thought that one day I might become one.

When I was 12, however, I experienced another big shock in my family life. One evening as she was praying, my grandmother became short of breath and passed away right in front of us. We couldn't believe what had happened and I felt tremendous pain in my heart.

After my grandmother's funeral, I insisted to all my family that I wanted to be with my mother in Venezuela. Reluctantly, my aunties and grandad agreed, and I went to live with them, while my brother, Carlos, stayed in Cali. However, neither of us were happy.

My stepfather and his family were kind to me, but I didn't feel that I belonged at home or at school. My mother and stepfather adopted a baby boy and, although I thought he was very sweet, I often felt left out and lonely. Outside of the home, I found the Venezuelan educational system to be challenging, and I struggled to make new friends in another country. The environment was drastically different from what I was used to and I felt increasingly disorientated in a foreign culture.

By my mid-teens, my mum and stepfather agreed that I should move back to my family in Cali and continue my studies there. One day, when I was 18, we received the terrible message that my lovely Mum, who had always continued to be a great support and best friend to me, had been involved in a car accident. At first, it seemed as though she would make a full recovery. Only a few hours later, however, she died as a result of internal bleeding that had not been detected. My grief consumed me. I did not know how to cope, and I couldn't stop crying. I couldn't get rid of my sadness. For a whole year I dressed in black. Despite my depression, somehow, I managed to finish my studies.

When I graduated from high school, I didn't want to go straight to university. Rather, I imagined that my best hope of future happiness was to get married as soon as possible and to raise a family. But that dream quickly came and went. I was just 24 when my husband and I split up after a difficult marriage. I was left with little support to bring up three young children; Carlos, the eldest, Jose, my second son, and my daughter, Lina, who was just 6 months old at the time.

I could feel bitterness taking over my heart. Inwardly, I resolved not to trust anyone anymore. From this point on I decided that I would do all that I could to provide for myself and my children. My mother's family supported me emotionally and helped me to be self-sufficient.

One aunty recommended me for an interview for a government job, which I was accepted for. Although the job was quite low paid, one big advantage was that I was eligible for a government sponsored scheme to study business administration for five years at a top university. I was so happy to have this opportunity even though it was often exhausting trying to juggle everything.

I would get up at 5 a.m. to go to university for my daily courses from 6.30 a.m. to 11 a.m. while I left the kids with a helper. Then I would go to my job in a government department before heading home to look after the children.

I finally graduated with high marks and began to set up different businesses. First, I had my own shop selling flowers, which are a specialty of Colombia. My first big customer was my university. Then I got involved in selling property and later became an advisor on interior design.

After a while, I decided that the best business opportunities were in Colombia's capital city. So, we moved to Bogotá where I set up my own insurance business. At the beginning, it was difficult to find clients as the market was highly competitive.

I had a busy life with many appointments. Even with some home-help however, it was very complicated and tiring being a single working mother. Of course, there were good times: nice meals out in smart restaurants, parties with friends, and holidays with my kids. I would try to take them to fun places like Disney World in Florida. But most of the time I felt we were just making it through life. I felt empty inside. There was no real joy or peace.

In my heart I longed for a normal family life and to be happily married. But I couldn't see how I could find the kind of man I was looking for. Deep down I knew I needed God's help, but I didn't know how to connect with Him. I had given up going to my traditional church, and I didn't know where else to turn.

Like many Colombians I was suspicious of having any contact with what we called "Evangelicos," enthusiastic, Bible-believing Christians who were growing so rapidly in Latin America.

One day however, I saw many people queuing to get into a large gospel church near my house and I thought I would check it out. I really was fully engaged as I listened to the preacher and liked his positive message. I also felt that it was a very warm atmosphere. So, I filled in a card to get connected but I didn't hear anything back. I even went to the office, but it was closed. So, I gave up and just continued with my life.

It was several years later that my next church connection came about. I started sharing about my life with my hair stylist, Yajaira Zutta. She was very friendly and listened sympathetically. She wasn't really supposed to talk about God in her workplace, but she said that what I really needed was to have Jesus in my life. She told me about her own experiences and invited me to her church.

I didn't know it at the time but her church, MCI (Misión Carismática Internacional or International Charismatic Mission), was one of the largest churches in the world, with over 100,000 members and many national and international branches. I told Yajaira that I appreciated her sincerity and concern for me, however I wanted to be clear with her that I was not interested in religion anymore. Despite my negative response, she was always friendly, and kept on inviting me whenever we met.

Finally, I thought, *"Why would I resist any longer? I've been searching for answers everywhere else, and I haven't found anything."* So, I told her I would come. When I actually turned up, she seemed shocked.

The first service I went to was held outdoors in the big Simón Bolívar Park. There were over 40,000 people there on that particular afternoon. The guest preacher was Pastor Omar Cabrera Junior from Argentina. I felt like he was talking directly to me. Even though I knew it wasn't possible, it seemed like my friend had somehow told him all about me.

This pastor spoke of a woman in the gospels who had suffered pain for many years and gone through many difficult circumstances. But she had reached out and touched Jesus and experienced a miraculous healing.

At one point in his message, he declared that there were women present who felt abandoned. Then he said these words: "God, has a paradise for you, the one you have dreamed of." To me it was incredible to hear this because that had been my childhood dream. This one sentence broke my heart.

For the first time in my life, I knew that God was speaking to me directly. Even though there were so many people around, I could feel His presence and above all, a warm and comforting love. It was like I had come home.

When the preacher said that "whoever would ask Jesus to come into their lives would know paradise," I too decided to reach out to God. I fell to my knees in that park, and I sobbed and sobbed. I couldn't stop. I asked God to heal me from all my pain and sadness. For the very first time ever, I felt that God had heard my prayer and was right by me. I felt totally different in my heart. I was now sure that God really had a paradise in store for me.

As I had knelt so long during the time of prayer, my friend couldn't see where I was. She assumed that I had not liked the service and had left. But then she saw me get up crying, with very messed up makeup, and she knew that God had touched my heart. We had a big hug.

I told Yajaira, "I want this. This is what I have been looking for. I want to be a member of this church. I want to come every day. What do I do?"

Since that very first moment, I really believed in God, and I fully committed my life to Him and immediately got involved in the church.

I would get up every day at 5 a.m. to pray and to read and study the Bible. I waited till 6 a.m. to call Yajaira to ask her to explain what different parts of the Scriptures meant. I had so many questions and was eager to learn. Yajaira told me later that I helped to train her as a leader as she had to get up early to prepare for my calls.

When I heard that this very big church was organised with many small groups, I wanted to be part of one. Yajaira helped me start a group in my house two weeks after I became a Christian. I invited as many people as I could. Ten of my friends and family came.

A month later Yajaira, who was so faithful in looking after me as a new Christian, came with me to a three-day event. It was called an Encounter Weekend and ran from Friday to Sunday. There were about 1000 new Christians there.

The church leaders had prayed and fasted for weeks for the people who would attend the encounter. Their prayers did not go unanswered as I felt God's presence in such a strong way that I spent most of the three days crying.

In that time, I came to have a totally new understanding of the power of Christ's suffering and His death on the cross. I experienced an even deeper healing in my heart from the many hurts of my life. I felt I was being washed clean from the bitterness of so many years. It was like I was being freed from prison. I was now confident that God had a new future for me and that the Holy Spirit would always help me live in a new way.

After that powerful encounter, I started attending every possible service that I could. I had the privilege of listening to many wonderful messages from Senior Pastor César Castellanos. I learnt so much from his teachings about truly living for God, being faithful, and always trusting God and His many promises in the Bible. It was practical, inspiring and not at all intense like I had imagined it would be.

One of the things that most impressed me was to see Pastor César's family with him both on and off stage. He was so close to his wife and his four daughters. They all obviously really loved each other. I saw the same good relationships in the families of all the pastors of our church and it really brought a new hope to me. This was so different to the dysfunctional family life that I had known.

Not surprisingly, I began to dream of new possibilities that I too could have a great marriage and a happy Christian family. I began praying for a genuine, faithful and romantic husband who really loved God and who would really love me.

All this was going on in my heart and mind when I attended my first international conference in El Campín Colosseum a few months later. I was impressed to see so many joyful people coming together from so many countries.

I particularly remember the first speaker. He was a guest pastor from England. From where I was, he was like a dot on the platform way below. I watched him mostly on the big screens, but from the first moment he spoke, he caught my attention.

He told an incredible story of how God had brought healing and restoration to him and his three children after his wife of many years had died. He was such a long way from me in that big auditorium, but his words and sincerity really reached my heart. They gave me great hope because I could relate to him as a single parent with three children who had also known a lot of hurt.

Even from where I was sitting, I could see very clearly that he was a very faithful man who had carried on serving God and his family for several years even without a wife to help him.

I thought that if God could help this man and his family, then maybe He could help our family too, and give us our own story of a new beginning.

As much as the British pastor's words touched me, I also could not help noticing that he was a very elegant man dressed in a smart blue suit. Obviously, he was from another culture and spoke a different language and this was the first time that I was even aware of his existence.

The likelihood of us ever connecting in any way seemed remote. Even so, I clearly remember thinking, *"One day I would love to meet and marry a man like that."*

CHAPTER 2
ADRIANA'S STORY: THE LONG WAIT FOR LOVE

In the days that followed the 2008 conference in Bogotá, I had increased faith that I could one day find the kind of husband that I was looking for. After many years of being cynical, I now believed that there were actually some good men out there, thanks in part to what I had seen and heard from the British pastor.

As far as he personally was concerned, he seemed like a dream to me but not one that was attainable. I felt confident, however, that God did have someone special for me. In the meantime, I thought the best thing that I could do was to prepare myself and pray for the day when I would meet and marry my ideal husband.

Like many other people in the church, I put together what we called a dream book. On the first page of my dream book I attached a photo of a bride with a bride's dress. I found a photo of mine and replaced the bride's face with my own. I wanted to have a strong visual image of what I was hoping for. I also wrote down a romantic text from the Song of Songs 7:10, "I belong to my lover and his desire is for me." Then I wrote out a prayer and a list of all that I hoped for in a husband.

Dear Father, Sovereign God. My dream for this year 2008 is to get married. I would like him to be like this:

- *That he has God's calling*
- *Tall*
- *Elegant*
- *Excellent manners*
- *Worshipper*
- *Prosperous*
- *That he has the heart of a pastor*
- *Happy and joyful*
- *Wise*
- *That He loves God with all his heart*
- *Mature in God*
- *Teachable heart*
- *Character shaped by God*
- *Intelligent*
- *Patient*
- *That he loves me and my children*

With the man God has for me as a husband and for my children as a father, I desire a stable home, happy, harmonious, prosperous, where all of us as a family are happy and that we love and honour God every day and together we serve God.

Even though I could clearly visualise the type of man I wanted in a husband, I wasn't at all clear about how to move from my dreams to the reality of seeing them fulfilled. Nor did I envisage how long that process might take, which was probably just as well as I didn't expect to wait for some years to see my dreams come to pass.

One day I read a verse from the Bible which I felt gave me some direction about how I could best prepare for the future. It was from Proverbs 24:27 which said, "Put your outdoor work in order and get your fields ready; after that, build your house." I understood this to mean that, first, I needed to get my business and finances in a good place. Then I considered what it meant to prepare the fields. My pastors told me that I should develop "fields of service" for God by growing as a leader and reaching out to people. "Building your house" meant to me that I would build a good home. I thought, *"Lord, so that's last? My marriage will come last?"*

I began to take action on this list of priorities and focused on building my insurance business. It was challenging to find new business in a competitive market. I worked long hours, often driving to another city several hours away. As I didn't have a husband to support me, I prayed that God's favour would be released over me in this time of singleness.

God answered my prayers, and my business began to grow and I won several large contracts insuring big lorries. It was not common for a woman to succeed in this sector. The bosses of companies, with whom I negotiated, were from a very macho culture. They often spoke roughly and rudely to me. Before I was a Christian, I would have been very forceful in my responses, but as I grew in my faith, the Lord helped me to be more patient.

As a result, I gained their respect and trust, and I won many lucrative contracts and commissions.

During this time of favour in my business, I always made a point of increasing my giving to the church; and as I did, I found that I received even more blessings. Not only did I see an increase in my finances, but I also won different awards and travel competitions. Many of these were from a big British insurance company. I was able to visit many places in South and Central America, the Caribbean, USA, Europe and Africa.

One of the best trips was to London for the Olympics in 2012. Everything was paid for. I went to the opening ceremony and attended the semifinals and finals of various events. We also enjoyed a day out in Windsor. I loved everything I saw: the Castle on the hill - the family home of British kings and queens for nearly 1,000 years - the river teeming with little boats and regal swans, the varied architecture reflecting the style of bygone eras, the old-fashioned pubs and streets, the very British train station, the traditional red phone boxes, and the displays of colourful flowers in the parks and outside many homes. It was all so beautiful and peaceful. I thought how special it must be to live in a place like this. I was aware that Pastor Wes lived in the area, but I had no reason to see him. Anyway, I would not have been able to speak to him in English even if I had met him.

Life carried on as usual back in Bogotá. Since I was my own boss and my children were now young adults, I was able to set my own schedule so that I had more time to pray, read my Bible, exercise in the morning and be involved in church services or activities most evenings.

ADRIANA'S STORY: THE LONG WAIT FOR LOVE

For seven years, and several times a week, I drove one hour, each way, to the church buildings - through Bogotá's notorious traffic - to receive great teaching and to be part of a positive atmosphere.

I also went to some of Bogotá's most needy and dangerous neighbourhoods to share the good news of Jesus. Although many people were not interested, I saw whole families, as well as individuals, giving their lives to God. I felt honoured to invest into the lives of these new believers, just as Yajaira had done with me. I helped them to develop as disciples and leaders. I would also host small groups in my home.

For me none of this was a pressure or a problem but a privilege. It was a way of saying "thank you" to God for all of His goodness and mercy to me.

As I focused on building my home, I prayed earnestly that my children would come to know the Lord. I was so encouraged when they each made their own decisions to follow Jesus. I still have the moving notes they wrote to me after they had their own experience with God at their encounter weekends. I loved that we could be together in church as a family.

I also started to feel that I should try to reconnect with another member of the family, my father. Since my last contact with him had been in Cali as a child, I began to search many telephone directories. I even called a few different numbers, but that didn't get me anywhere. So, I decided to go on a direct search for him when I went to Cali for Christmas with my kids.

On New Year's Eve 2011, we drove to an area where I remembered my dad's sister used to live. I had hoped that I would be able to recognise her house. Unfortunately, as we travelled around, all the different neighbourhoods and houses looked the same, and I was unable to figure out where she lived.

I prayed for the Holy Spirit to guide me. Not long after, when I saw two older women talking on a street, I had a strong feeling that I should stop the car and speak to them. I told them who I was looking for and gave them the name of my aunty. After questioning me briefly, one of the ladies told me to wait while she went inside her house. It turned out that although my aunty had moved away, this lady still had her phone number. She returned to say that she had just contacted her and that my aunty had asked for me to call her.

When I rang, I was very happy to hear my aunty's warm and friendly voice on the other end of the line. She invited me to come to her house and said that she was sure that my dad would want to hear from me. When we arrived at her house, she told me that my dad was recovering from a heart attack and that we needed to be careful that he would not be overwhelmed. Together, she and I dialled his number. I still remember standing next to her as she suggested to my dad that he "sit down and relax" because she had "good news" for him about a surprise visitor. Immediately he said, "It's Adriana, isn't it?" and then she handed the phone to me.

I simply said, "Hi Papa, it's Adriana, how are you?" He immediately said how pleased he was to hear my voice and shared how he had spent considerable time looking for me over the years. We both started crying and had an emotional conversation. Then we agreed to meet up that afternoon.

My kids and aunties were with me when my dad walked into the room where we were waiting. I felt nervous after not having seen him for thirty-five years. But as soon as my dad saw me, he came quickly towards me with his arms outstretched. He kissed me on my cheek and hugged me tightly. He was crying. I was crying. Everyone in the room was crying. When we had all regained our composure, he said again that he had tried many times to get in touch with me but had not been able to. I said that all that mattered now was that we were back together. I was then introduced to his other family. I found that I had a stepmother and two half-brothers who were all kind-hearted towards my kids and myself.

That night they all agreed to come with us to a New Year's Eve service with the Cali branch of my church. My dad sat next to me and held my hand throughout the service. I reflected on how God had, yet again, answered my prayers and brought more restoration in my life. All this increased my faith to continue to pray for another missing person to come into my life… my future husband.

I continued to do my best to get ready for him. I went to the gym every day around 7 a.m. I lifted weights, took spinning classes, ran on the treadmill and visualised my future husband as I did so. I kept to a strict diet and cut out as many carbohydrates as I could. Not having bread was a big deal for me with all my childhood memories in a bakery. But I didn't mind the sacrifice as I focused on being in the best shape for my future husband.

I also bought new clothes to look more elegant. I made sure I kept up with manicures and pedicures and made regular visits to the local hair salon.

Once, I had the bright idea that I would try to follow the Biblical example of Esther. Before her marriage she had "to complete twelve months of beauty treatments prescribed for the women, six months with oil of myrrh and six with perfumes and cosmetics."[1] I therefore started collecting various brands of oils and perfumes. Some of them were so strong that one colleague joked that she always knew when I was in the office as she could smell me as soon as she entered the building. I bought a lot of creams for my skin and face which I applied, without fail, every morning and evening. I combined all of these personal rituals with my family life, my business, and my church involvement. Seriously, I was on a mission in every way.

I was as ready as I could possibly be to meet my Prince Charming. I was full of anticipation. But what happened? Nothing. Absolutely nothing. There was still no sign of my long-awaited husband.

Every year I thought *"this is my year,"* only to discover that it wasn't. I began to feel depressed. I battled with feelings of loneliness as well as doubts and fears that I would ever find the husband I was looking for. I cried a lot during this long season of waiting. *"Oh Lord, how much longer?"*

---

1. Esther 2:12

I tried to keep faith for my future husband as I saw many people in the church getting married, including some of my friends, and I often helped to serve at their weddings. It was hard not to wonder whether I was setting my sights too high, especially as I was getting older and was now a grandmother. Even one of my good friends told me to be *"more realistic."* I decided, however, that although it wasn't easy, I would not give up on my dreams. I continued to believe that God was working for my good even though I couldn't see anything happening.

I kept on praying. I found it easy to identify with the story of the persistent widow in the Bible, which Jesus used to teach his disciples that, "they should always pray and never give up."[2]

At different times I received offers from guys, both from inside and outside of the church, to go on dates with them. Some promised a very prosperous future. However, I decided not to start a relationship with any man who wasn't fully committed to God. I didn't want to make any mistakes, so I sought the protection of my leaders by asking anyone interested in me to "please talk with my pastors." Well, that certainly weeded out anyone who wasn't serious. In fact, my approach worked so effectively that I never began any romantic relationships as my pastors watched out for me. You really need to have a high level of confidence in your pastors' discernment when that keeps happening!

One day, my immediate pastor, Pastor Doris Villar-

---

2. Luke 18:1

whose husband was reassuringly called Pastor Jesus (a common name in Colombia) had a heart-to-heart chat with me. She said, "Adriana, I don't believe your husband is here in Bogotá or in Colombia. God has somebody very special for you. He has a man of God from another nation already being prepared for you. You must just keep serving and waiting in faith for the right time when he will come into your life. You have been faithful to God and He will be faithful to you."

Around this time another pastor, Ligia Zuluaga, came up to me at the end of a powerful night of prayer attended by many thousands of people. She said that God had shown her that I was like Ruth in the Bible who had remained faithful as a single woman in difficult circumstances. In the right moment, she suddenly met and then married Boaz. She said that my "Boaz" would come for me.

On another occasion, Pastor Emma Claudia Castellanos said something similar referring to another Bible character: "Adriana you are like Rebekah. She was a beautiful single lady who was just going about her daily life when suddenly everything changed, and she quickly became the wife of Isaac."

All these messages encouraged me to stay steady in my faith. I believed that these words from my spiritual leaders would one day turn out to be true.

Every year, as I was waiting for my husband to come into my life, I continued to attend the annual international conference in Bogotá. As I did, I became more aware of Pastor Wes who was often a guest speaker. I felt a growing connection with him as I heard him share more about his life and his growing family. I identified with many things he said, and his words always touched my heart.

As the years went by, I was amazed to find out that he had never remarried. Often men who are widowed marry again very quickly. I was impressed that he hadn't rushed into another marriage after losing his wife.

By 2015, I had become increasingly interested in the possibility of meeting him. I began to think that, perhaps, Pastor Wes should be on my radar as a potential husband. I even confided to a friend over dinner, "I really like this pastor. He's very interesting."

Not long afterwards, at the January 2015 conference, a woman pastor, who did not know of this conversation, said she thought it would be good if I could meet Pastor Wes. She knew my daughter was planning to study in England, and she thought that he would probably be willing to help. At the end of one service, she led me to the front seats of the auditorium to introduce me to him. However, as we came near to where he was, I could see he was busy praying for someone. I felt uncomfortable standing there, so I asked the pastor not to worry about trying to arrange a meeting and we walked away. It simply didn't seem to be coming together to meet Pastor Wes.

In the summer of that year, my good friend Pastor Yolanda Almanza de Rodriguez, heard that I was about to go to England to help my daughter, Lina, get settled in a university. She said that she would ask her grandson, Pastor Andrew, who was a friend of Pastor Wes, to make a connection for us. She believed that Pastor Wes would be willing to advise us. She soon got back to me to say that Pastor Wes had agreed to have an appointment with us in his office in Windsor.

As a mother, I felt a sense of relief that someone would be able to support me with Lina's move to the UK. I was also happy at the prospect of another summer visit to the beautiful royal town of Windsor. What most excited me, however, was that now, nearly seven years after Pastor Wes's words of hope and healing had first touched my heart, I was finally going to meet him personally. I couldn't wait to pack!

CHAPTER 3
WES'S STORY: SLOWLY WAKING UP TO NEW POSSIBILITIES

As Adriana made her way carefully down from the top of the Colosseum in 2008, I had no idea that I had made a favourable impression on a very lovely lady from Colombia.

Once the conference sessions finished, I stepped outside onto the large concourse with my family, which was, in fact, very close to the exit from where Adriana, a total stranger to me, was leaving the arena. I wrote in the final paragraph of my book *Hope and a Future*: "I left the coliseum with hugs from my family and holding my grandsons." Then, quoting Psalm 121 I added, "I lifted my eyes to the beautiful hills around Bogotá. And I smiled."

Over the next seven years there were more smiles as I returned to Bogotá for the annual international conferences which were an ever-increasing inspiration to me and the ministry of our church. I was frequently asked to speak during this time. As I did, I was in total ignorance of Adriana, who faithfully attended the conferences, and that she was feeling a growing connection with me. So, with Adriana and romance nowhere on my horizon, I would return home every year trying to move forward as best as I could with my life as a single pastor, father and grandfather.

Thankfully, the memories of my first years of facing the volatile stages of grief continued to fade. I had received a powerful healing of my heart, especially after Pastor César had wept over me as he prayed for me on my first conference visit. I certainly felt the comfort of God through him which helped me greatly as I slowly built a new life without my beloved Carol. Emerging from my own and my family's time of darkness, however, was not the same as wanting to get married again. I don't think that I ever dismissed the possibility of discovering love again, but I couldn't see how that could practically happen, and it was never a priority.

I never viewed myself as a "poor, lost widower." Instead, I simply recognised that I had re-joined most of the world in living as a "single." It was not all bad and sad. Far from it. In many ways, I was enjoying life. I recognised the freedom that I had as a single person, and I was determined to count every blessing.

I had more time to focus on being the senior pastor of King's Church International, a great community of people from over 50 nations located in Windsor, UK. I was increasingly thankful that, back in my mid 20's, I had chosen to leave my career as an evening newspaper journalist. At the time, it appeared to some of my colleagues as a mystifying decision. But over the years I felt increasing fulfilment in serving God in my home church, which had been started during the Second World War by my late father, Billy Richards, a former Welsh coal miner.

His life, his legacy, and his teachings, together with memories of the faithful example of my deceased mother, Marian, encouraged me to persevere in all circumstances. No doubt, all this kept me anchored and purpose-driven in my own times of trouble and transition.

I didn't have too much time to think about my own personal future or to sit around and mope even if I had been tempted to. I lived a very full life not only as a pastor, but also as a speaker at different large conferences around the world as part of the international ministry of Pastor César Castellanos. It was always so motivating to be with him and to discover, at close quarters, how he lived out his faith and kept close to his family. All this he managed to do with great grace as he led a fast-growing global Christian network that was focussed on following the example of Jesus by building and multiplying teams of 12 committed disciples. I also valued the camaraderie with great pastors from other nations.

Additionally, I travelled to South Africa three times each year to give direction and support to King's Church International in Robertson in the Western Cape, which we had started in 2009, and where a new strong multi-racial, non-traditional Christian community and leadership team was steadily building. It involved a lot of vision casting, practical Bible teaching, ongoing prayer, home visits, and many personal conversations. Yet, for all the hard work, it was inspiring to see change coming from the ground up. I was also greatly encouraged that we were regularly ministering help, hope, and healing to over 1000 children and young people, many of whom had experienced abuse of different kinds.

Like my father before me, I had long believed in the importance of ministry to children, something Jesus Himself had so clearly prioritised and which I could confirm from my own personal experience.

I became a Christian at just five years of age, not through the ministry of a famous evangelist like Billy Graham, but thanks to a children's puppet show that our church was hosting. I can clearly remember one of the puppets asking if any boys and girls wanted to give their lives to Jesus. Even though my young age meant that I didn't need to repent of a long list of sins and crimes, I can recall feeling happy when I "asked Jesus into my heart."

The simple teaching that Jesus was my best friend helped me greatly three years later when I became seriously ill with peritonitis. My parents were warned by the doctors that I may not be alive by the next day. I remember being in so much pain that I prayed, "Jesus heal me or bring me to heaven. I can't stand this." That night there was a special prayer meeting for me.

A single, older Welsh lady, called Christie Jones, petitioned God "to save the life of this little boy and one day use him as a preacher." My mother said that it was like Christie opened the gates of heaven as she prayed and, in those moments, my parents felt sure that I had been healed. In fact, as bewildered doctors later confirmed, it was indeed at that very time, that my dangerously high temperature had suddenly and unaccountably dropped, and my condition stabilised.

Now, many years after my sudden recovery, Christie Jones's prayer was being answered in an increasing number of places and in different ways. In addition to our ministry in South Africa, we were also involved with Burkina Faso, one of the world's poorest countries, where we have supported several schools and charitable projects for over 30 years.

Back at home base, I had my hands full as we embarked on an ambitious venture to help the next generation by starting a new school, The King's House School, Windsor, in the autumn of 2012. This had been a personal goal ever since I held my first two grandsons in my arms and considered the kind of world that they had been born into. I felt a responsibility to give them, and their contemporaries, a strong foundation for life based on a Christian worldview.

I wanted to pioneer a school that would enable children to develop in a positive environment and to grow "in wisdom and stature, and in favour with God and man," as Luke 2:52 puts it. This vision meant taking a big step of faith. As I announced at the time, we had everything in place to start the school, "except a building, pupils, teachers, curriculum, finances and permission." In less than nine months, however, it all came together after a lot of prayer, trust in God, and remarkable teamwork, organised by my daughter, Melody, and supported by a talented team of specialists and 12 core families. It was soon commended by Ofsted, the British government's educational regulatory body.

One of the reasons that the school grew numerically was that our family helped to populate it. When *Hope and a Future* was published, I dedicated it, "to Carol for her love, life and legacy… and the grandchildren who came after her: Samuel, Joseph, Joshua, Joel, Isaac, Daniel, Caleb, Eliana and…" Well, those dots were prophetic. Five more grandchildren were to follow, including three more girls to keep Eliana company.

The dots became names and very special individual personalities. My ninth grandchild was David Wesley Jacobus Richards who was born to Wesley and Wilana on January 12, 2013. He was followed by Grace Carolina Erasmus born to Melody and Drikus on December 21, 2013, and Marianna Joy Richards born to James and Esther[1] on October 31, 2014.

Each one was dedicated to the Lord at an early age. Each of them pulled on my heart in a special way. They were all a big focus of my prayers, which were particularly necessary for Grace. When she was just three months old, her oxygen levels dropped suddenly and alarmingly. She was quickly taken into a special care unit in a local hospital where she was diagnosed with Tetralogy of Fallows, a complex heart defect affecting 6 in 10,000 babies. Although no one knew it at the time, this was the start of a very traumatic four weeks as Mel and Drikus' little daughter's life hung in the balance.

Our church family, locally and globally, rallied round

---

1. Esther changed her name from Vasti (Afrikaans for Vashti) in 2020.

us all. One afternoon, while I anointed Grace with oil, Pastor César prayed a powerful prayer over the internet. He encouraged us to visualise a miracle, to believe for a blessed life for Grace, and for favour in the trial she was currently facing.

Grace's deteriorating condition meant that she needed a four-hour emergency open-heart bypass surgery at London's Great Ormond Street Hospital, one of the world's top children's hospitals. After what seemed to us an eternity, it was a great relief when the doctors emerged to announce that the operation had been a success. Grace needed to stay another week in a high-dependency unit where the medical staff could monitor her closely. I, too, spent a lot of time in the hospital supporting her parents and prayerfully watching over Grace at her bedside.

We all emerged from this month of testing with a strengthened faith and thanks for God's *Amazing Grace,* as well as our own little amazing Grace.

And so, as the years rolled by, I laughed a lot with my grandchildren and with my "kids" as I saw them face the many challenges of parenting very different personalities. There was more joy to come when Drikus and Mel, with three children aged five and under, including the now healthy Grace, told me that they were expecting again. The scan pictures soon revealed not one but two babies in the womb. After all their troubles, double blessings were coming their way and ours. Twins, Keziah Faith Ann Erasmus and then, 20 minutes later, Josiah Johannes Ephraim Erasmus, were born healthy and happy on July 6, 2015.

My status as a grandfather was now well and truly established with 13 grandchildren. I felt happy to have been around for all the births and to have been able to support all my kids with all their kids. But it appeared from my inquiries that the "baby factory" was now closed, and everybody, with their hands full, was moving forward in establishing their lives, families and careers.

We were all still close, yet I felt that this was a moment for me not only to look back with gratitude, but also to consider what the future might look like for me personally. I sensed that change was coming, and I believed that, even with the passing years, the best times could still be ahead. As I was about to discover, the summer of 2015 was indeed the time when a new season of life was dawning. Events that could have happened at different moments but didn't happen were now about to unfold.

For some time, different friends of mine had told me of their very clear ideas about what the future would look like for me. They were all convinced that I should and would marry again. Over the years, wherever I travelled, various well-meaning pastors and other friends tried to persuade me to find a bride. If I had listened to all of their suggestions, I would have had multiple wives by now!

My long-time friend, Mike Peters, would give me an "annual check-up" on my marital prospects when I spent time with him and his wife, Linda, at their home in St. Louis during the summer holidays. This "check-up" usually entailed Pete outlining all my options as he saw them. Did I want to marry someone older, younger, my age, previously married, never married, British, American, South African, new Christian, veteran Christian, blonde, brunette, redhead…? I felt both exhausted and amused just listening to all the different choices that I apparently needed to make. It was like trying to order a salad in an American restaurant with endless dressing options.

Pete, a Doctor of Divinity, was so rigorous in his research that I thought he could have almost written another dissertation on the subject. However, seeing that I was not altogether receptive, Pete would conclude that we should just relax and make the most of each moment. This usually meant that we would spend as much time as possible visiting Busch Stadium to watch the St. Louis Cardinals baseball team.

Linda, however, was not so easily dissuaded. What's more, on one visit she shared with me one morning that she had had a clear dream of a dark-haired lady whom she felt would be my future wife. I didn't really know what to say to that, but I thanked her politely and pondered what it might mean.

One of the most persistent campaigners for me getting married again was another American friend, Bray Sibley, a multi-talented, preacher, blues-singer, songwriter, keyboard player from the Deep South. In addition to all these very obvious gifts he possessed, he wanted me to know, with all due humility, that he was also an expert matchmaker.

He once walked the entire length of The Long Walk in Windsor, a nearly 3-mile stretch, trying to draw out of me what type of lady I would like to marry before even checking whether or not I even wanted to remarry. He was very sure that I should start on my own "Long Walk to Freedom" from a single lifestyle. He proceeded to enthusiastically "present his case" to me as to why I should remarry. Some of his arguments focused on how happy I might be or how rich I might become. I gathered that these benefits were not necessarily to be found in the same person. Nonetheless, he was confident that he had all the angles covered.

His clearly embarrassed wife, Diane, who frequently rolled her eyes during her husband's quest to end my single status, laughed when he finally had to quit in defeat as I evaded all of his questions. In retrospect, however, I can see now that my go-getting American buddy's arguments were not completely lost on me. He had, in fact, got me thinking that maybe I should be more open to the prospect of getting married again.

Another nudge in this direction came from Pastor Jorge Andres "Andrew" Cataño. In addition to his gifts as a speaker and translator, he too was ready to fire Cupid's arrows.

At the UK conference in June 2015, he tried to establish my interest in a beautiful lady leader from his church. He said her name was Adriana Bastidas and that he and his wife thought that I should meet her. He told me some of her story and suggested that I should seriously consider letting him arrange an introduction. To my surprise, he then opened his phone and showed me some attractive Facebook pictures of Adriana and her family. He looked me in the eyes and asked with a hint of triumph in his voice, "Are you sure you don't want to meet her?" I kept a straight face and told him to put away his mobile and to stay focussed on his mission at hand as he was the next conference speaker.

Although I didn't let him know it at the time, Andrew had succeeded in lodging in my mind a pleasant first impression of the lady in question. When I arrived home, I hereby freely confess that I checked out her Facebook profile. I was startled to discover that somewhere along the line I had already accepted Adriana as a friend, something I had done with hundreds of other fellow members of her church in Bogotá. I found myself smiling as I thought, *"So this beautiful lady in the photos knows all about me and had asked to be my friend. Interesting…"*

A few weeks later, after his informal and seemingly unproductive promotional campaign for Adriana, Andrew called me from Colombia saying that he had a formal request to make of me. His grandmother, Pastor Yolanda Almanza de Rodriguez, had asked him for a favour for a close friend of hers. The friend in question just happened to be the very same Adriana Bastidas that he had tried to earlier bring to my attention.

He told me that, in all seriousness, his grandma thought that it would be good if I could help Adriana. Her daughter, Lina, was coming to the UK for the autumn term as part of her studies in aeronautical engineering. To prepare for her move, they would soon both be arriving in England in early August. He asked if I would be willing to advise them and help them find somewhere suitable to stay while they were visiting.

This was more familiar and comfortable territory to me since we have long had a culture of hospitality in our church and family. So, I agreed to meet Adriana, my newly discovered Facebook friend, and her daughter Lina, simply out of pastoral concern and professional care… At least that's what I tried to convince myself.

CHAPTER 4
MEETING UP AT LAST

To prepare for the imminent arrival of Adriana and Lina, I asked my senior assistant, Terry Beasley, to arrange some accommodation in Windsor. I also asked him to make sure a nice hospitality basket and some flowers were available in their room, complete with a note of welcome. "Be sure to sign it on behalf of the church and not in my name" I added, just to avoid creating any wrong impressions.

Terry, my trusted friend since school days who had supported me through all seasons of life, then went to collect Adriana and Lina from Heathrow Airport. I was a little surprised that he felt he needed to call me on the brief journey back. I could hear Spanish being rapidly spoken in the background as he whispered conspiratorially, "Just thought you should know, Wes, that they have safely arrived, and that Adriana is beautiful." In retrospect, I can see that Terry did not think that he was picking up a random Colombian visitor who would have no further contact with us.

For her part, Adriana thought that this VIP-like welcome was an answer to prayer. She said:

After our meeting had been arranged, my friend, pastor Yolanda called a prayer group of older pastors to pray for our trip to England and that I would find favour in my first meeting with Pastor Wes. They certainly saw the romantic potential of our visit and prayed with a lot of faith and passion for me.

I was even more encouraged before leaving to learn that of all the churches in the UK that had connections with our church, it was Pastor Wes's church which was nearest to where Lina would be studying at Cranfield University. Consequently, for a time, he would be my daughter's pastor. I felt a sense of peace and expectation even before we landed.

From the beginning we felt like honoured guests. We were very well looked after, and everyone was very kind.

When we got to our room, I was so impressed to see a lovely welcome basket with chocolates, fruit, biscuits and juices along with some nice flowers. I was even more impressed when I read the card with a special message of welcome. It was not a general greeting but a personal message from Pastor Wes Richards. I kept re-reading that card!

Adriana and I were scheduled to meet not long after she and Lina had settled in. I was unaware of the positive impression that I had already made on Adriana since she had arrived, thanks to Terry deciding to do his old friend a favour by personalising the welcome note. I also had no idea of the efforts Adriana was making to prepare for our first meeting. She recalled:

To get ready for our appointment I had my hair blow-dried. I carefully applied my make-up and put on a beautiful dress. I walked with Lina to the church office in flat shoes, but when we came near, I stopped to change into high heels. Lina asked me what I was doing. I just smiled and told her that it was always important to look elegant at appointments.

Well, I can confirm that Adriana certainly achieved her goal. When she and Lina came into my office, I could see that Terry and Pastor Andrew had not exaggerated their descriptions of her. My first impression was of a beautiful lady, immaculately dressed and seemingly confident in an unfamiliar setting. She was very natural in her manner, and it soon became very evident that she was also a good mum who wanted the best for her daughter.

From the first, it was easy to talk with her, albeit with translation. I was happy to do what I could to help her and Lina. After what I thought was a positive 45 minutes, we had a prayer that everything would work out well and then we parted with warm good wishes.

After Adriana left however, I saw no reason for any more personal follow up conversations. Undoubtedly, she was charming and even more beautiful in person than in her Facebook photos, but she still was a virtual stranger from a foreign culture whose language I didn't speak. It had been pleasant to meet her but why would we need to remain in contact now that Lina had been introduced?

As soon as she left, I was much more focussed on completing my appointments so that I could return home and pack to go away the next day with some of my family.

Adriana's recollections of the meeting in my office revealed that, in total contrast to me, she was far more awakened than I was to the potential of our first meeting, which was hardly surprising given all the prayer that was going on in Colombia. Further, she did have the undoubted advantage of feeling she had some sort of connection with me after having heard me speak on different occasions. Plus, she had received a very personal and encouraging note of welcome which she had no reason to believe was not from me.

Adriana recalled:

When Pastor Wes welcomed us, he was very kind. I was trying not to make it too obvious, but I was very happy to meet him personally after seeing him at conferences for many years. I felt very relaxed and was eager to see what would happen. We had a good talk. He listened carefully and was very interested and helpful. He prayed for us in a moving way and then, as we were going, he just said, "Goodbye and God bless you" and that was that.

When we left and I had changed out of my high heels, I was feeling as flat as my shoes. After all the prayers and expectations, it seemed like a big anti-climax. There was nothing more to indicate that there could be anything that would develop between us.

I concluded that he hadn't seemed to notice me in any romantic way at all. Also, I thought that it was significant that he still had a picture of his late wife in his office. I thought that maybe this showed that he still hadn't got past his loss of many years before. I thought to myself, "Ah what a nice pastor. He's so kind but I don't think he wants to fall in love again." So, I left with admiration for him, but accepted that I was going to have to keep on praying for my dream husband.

I didn't tell anyone how disappointed I was about this meeting except my cousin Vicky from Cali who lived in London with her family. I said "Oh, I met this pastor and I really like him. But he's just not interested. He didn't even notice me as a woman he might be interested in."

But Vicky told me to relax. She said, "Don't lose your hope Adriana. If he is the one for you, one day the Lord will move his heart, and something will happen." That helped me a lot.

As Vicky was trying to reassure the somewhat downcast Adriana, I on the other hand was in high spirits preparing to go to France with my eldest son, Wesley, my daughter-in-law, Wilana, and their four young, energetic sons.

To be able to have quality time with members of my family was one of the big blessings of my single life. In the 13 years since Carol had died, I had always found holidays the most difficult to deal with, as life temporarily lost its usual structure and there was more opportunity to reflect on the realities of being a long-established widower. I never wanted to be a spare part, so I was always grateful that my family, in various combinations, would welcome me to join them as I always had fun hanging out with my kids and grandkids.

On this trip, to help preserve the sanity of the parents and build some memories between grandad and grandsons, we divided up the kids on the long drive down to the Bordeaux region. They took the more boisterous younger two, Daniel, then 4, and David, 2. Samuel, 8, Joshua, 6, came with me. They were very excited about this. They urged me to overtake their parents' slower vehicle at regular intervals and shouted triumphantly whenever we did so.

I suddenly felt years younger, and the long hours of driving passed quickly. I told them many stories, personal stories, family stories, and Bible stories. They told me about their friends and school experiences. We swapped jokes and I introduced them to the enduring popularity of Abba songs, not just worship songs or classical music that they were possibly expecting.

With the sun shining ever brighter as we made our way south, we sang along to such favourites as Mamma Mia, Take a Chance on Me and the Latin themed Chiquitita. In hindsight, I can see that there may have possibly been a subliminal reason why some of these songs were resonating with me. Maybe they were not unconnected to the Latin lady whom I had just met and who was herself about to go on holiday in Europe with her daughter and friends, including a visit to Paris.

I didn't know any details of the rest of Adriana's trip nor that they would be returning to Windsor while I was still in France.

Just before she went back to Colombia, Adriana accompanied Lina on her first visit to King's Church International, her new church in Windsor. Adriana said:

I felt the atmosphere in the church was very much like we were used to in Bogotá. I felt relieved that my daughter would be cared for in a church like this. From the moment we arrived we were given a very warm welcome by different people who didn't know anything about us. Pastor Margaret, wife of Pastor Terry, was very kind to us and made us feel very much at home. Also, Pastor Wes's daughter, Melody, was very kind and offered to look out for Lina.

Margaret recalled:

I remember Adriana being introduced to me as Lina's mum. I found her to be very friendly and she was obviously a beautiful lady. Adriana couldn't speak much English, but she certainly conveyed warmth and had a lovely smile. She seemed very happy to be with us all in the Windsor church. It was only later when my husband shared more about Adriana, that I thought "Oh, this could be interesting." I always felt that our friend and pastor, Wes, would get married again to a strong woman of God who would really love him.

Melody remembered:

My first meeting with Adriana was at the end of the service. I didn't really have much time to speak or even think properly because I was pretty sleep deprived at that moment with newborn twins. But I was awake enough to register that she was a warm person as well as a very elegant lady. I think I was more focussed on getting to know Lina who, we found out, was the girlfriend of our Colombian friend, Raul, an intern in the church for several years. He had become a close part of our family whilst staying in the UK. When her mum went home, I realised that we really needed to get closer to Lina and look after her.

At a party a few weeks later, I could see that Lina was struggling being with a group of people she didn't know and was trying to keep to herself. She was obviously very homesick, so I gave her a hug. I thought that she was very sincere, and that I should figure out what I could do to help her.

Back over in France, completely unaware of new connections that were being made at home, I took some time out to process where I was at with my life and what I really wanted for the future. My thoughts came into sharper perspective on one sunny evening. Wesley and Wilana needed to get the boys to bed early and so we agreed to go our separate ways for a few hours.

I went for a drive to the nearby picturesque medieval town of St-Emilion, home of some of France's most famous and expensive vineyards. I parked up and was soon exploring the ancient, cobbled streets in one of UNESCO's outstanding World Heritage sites. There was a slight breeze, the sky was blue, and the air was almost literally intoxicating. Different groups of families and friends were enjoying the sunshine, chatting and laughing at pavement cafés. Older couples strolled contentedly along together. Young lovers walked by slowly, arms wrapped around each other, pausing only to kiss, oblivious to everyone else.

I was cheered to witness so much simple *joie de vivre* and thankful to have the mobility and opportunity to walk freely around in this little paradise on this perfect summer evening. Yet, at the same time, I felt a sadness trying to creep up on me which I was struggling to resist.

I knew of course that I would not be alone for long and that I would soon be back with my family. I also realised that plenty of other people experienced similar sensations of feeling totally alienated in a crowd. All the same, there was no denying an inner emotional ache. It was something I had learned to get used to. Yet, on this wonderful evening, a long way from normal home routines and church life, I sensed that maybe it didn't always have to be like this and that this was as good an opportunity as any for some very honest self-reflection.

I walked away from the crowds to a high vantage point above the town with its picture-book panoramic views of the French countryside. I found an old stone wall to sit on and tried to evaluate what was going on in my head and heart and what kind of future I envisaged. I thought about all the amazing and comforting developments that had happened in our family since we had experienced such grief with the death of Carol. I reflected that she and I could have easily been sitting here together enjoying the maturity of our marriage like many of the other couples whom I had seen that evening. But it was not to be. I still missed her of course, but my time of mourning had ended many years before.

I considered whether it was even realistic to get married again and find new happiness. I realised that plenty of people had remarried and known a deep marital love once more, but in my case, as so many years had now passed by, I wondered whether it was too late to meet that special someone. I was not 21 anymore, not even 61. I couldn't imagine how on earth there could come new romance and a second marriage in my busy life. And anyway, in my heart of hearts, did I really want to start all over again to build a new relationship? That might be too demanding.

Yes, I did not like the loneliness that I experienced from time to time, such as on this balmy night in this romantic place. But most of the time, thankfully, I wasn't depressed, just empty sometimes. I had become well-practised at managing the reoccurring emotions that came with recognizing that something, or rather someone, was missing in my life.

I focused on counting all of my blessings: my large family, my friends, the church, and diverse opportunities to minister in many places to many people. Maybe I could achieve far more as a single Christian leader, as the apostle Paul had outlined as a worthy option? Being single, I concluded, had many compensations. So maybe the best plan really was just to get on with life and make the most of each day. Keep calm and carry on.

After having had this thorough debate with myself, I decided that the possibilities and practical realities of ever getting married again all seemed a bit too complicated to dwell on. And anyway, despite my cordial meeting with Adriana, I was not focussed on any potential candidate. But something must have been moving me to being more open to a new romance because I had enough faith to pray, even though admittedly it was somewhat half-hearted:

Lord if you have got a wife out there for me then you will have to make it obvious to me and to sort it out. You arranged it last time very well. So, you are my best hope of finding someone this time. But a new wife would really have to love you, love me and love my family. Oh yes... and one more thing… I would also really appreciate, Lord, it if she was seriously beautiful.

My prayers and thoughts then abruptly returned to the present when the very loud bells of the famous 12th century Monolithic church chimed eight times. I got up to return to our quaint rented farmhouse to prepare supper for my son and daughter-in-law.

Little did I know that, not even a year later, I would again be on holiday in very different circumstances with a new member of my family. Sooner than I realised, I was about to be surprised by love.

CHAPTER 5
AND NOW IT BEGINS

As the summer ended and autumn nights drew in, Adriana was back in Colombia reflecting on a trip to England that was far less romantic than she had hoped for. I continued in my ignorance of her romantic interest in me. There were no plans to meet up again. So that was that. Or so it seemed.

But the doors for any further interaction between us were not as closed as it appeared. An unexpected development now emerged that would open the way for further contact. For Lina, having now started her university term in the UK, was not settled in her student accommodation. Learning of this, Melody, having already seen how homesick Lina was, had a proposal to put to me. She thought it could be a win/win for everyone. Melody and Drikus had continued to live with me which was a great blessing for us all, but now we were all feeling home life was too hectic.

Melody suggested, "Dad it's been crazy since the

twins arrived, so we could do with some extra backup. What do you think about Lina living with us? She would really benefit from being with a family. And, since she doesn't have to be on campus most of the time, we could give her free accommodation, and she could help us with the kids and around the house."

I quickly agreed and within days Lina moved in and immediately slotted into our busy lives. Melody remembers:

Lina and I soon became good friends. We were often in stressful situations with babies screaming and kids jumping off the furniture. You have to get to know each other very quickly. I was really impressed with her. She never seemed stressed. She was always calm and willing to help. She was also great fun, and the kids loved her. However, she wouldn't allow them to beat her at Super Mario Cart. She became like a sister.

I also quickly formed a favourable impression of Lina as I got to know her, as we constantly loaded and unloaded the dishwasher and cleared up after meals. Lina was easy-going, keen to help, and had a quirky sense of humour. We all liked her. In fact, oddly, she felt like part of the family.

She began to tell us about her own home background. Her mum was obviously a heroine to her, having brought up three kids by herself, run her own business, and supported Lina in her university ambitions. She told us how her mum had become a committed and faithful Christian and how her prayers and example had brought a lot of help and change in Lina's own life.

"At first we gave Mum a hard time to see if her new faith was real," she said. "We would try to provoke her in her reactions. We said that if she reacted badly to us, we would go and tell her pastors! Before long we realised that mum really was different, and so I wanted what she had."

I was impressed by the honouring way Lina spoke about her mum. I could see the great job she had obviously done in raising such a well-balanced and sincere daughter.

I didn't want to betray my rising interest, so I didn't ask many questions. However, I thought that it wouldn't cause too many problems if I made a few innocent inquiries such as whether or not her mum was a good cook… Ok, not so innocent.

Lina explained that they had a housekeeper who usually prepared meals for them, omitting to add that her mum was an excellent cook. Unknown to me, our conversation was casually relayed back by Lina to her mum. She was apparently not impressed with her daughter's reply to me. Adriana recalled:

After thinking that the door had closed for any future connection with Pastor Wes, I had been happily surprised to hear that my daughter was now actually living in his home. I thought 'Well now perhaps he can know a bit more about me and hopefully have a good impression of me.' When Lina told me that he had asked her whether I could cook I thought 'Oh, maybe he does have some interest in me after all.' But I couldn't believe Lina's reply. I remember saying to her "Lina, why didn't you tell him I can cook well?"

I thought 'Well, perhaps the opportunity was lost.' I was still praying for my husband and wondering 'perhaps it's Pastor Wes, perhaps it's not.'

Just before Christmas the chastened Lina returned to Colombia having completed her term in the UK, to receive the forgiving embrace of her Mum and, no doubt, to enjoy some of her quality meals. I sent a Christmas card to Adriana and family via Lina with a few warm but rather general seasonal greetings.

During the holidays, as we focussed on the New Year, each of my children began asking me about my own thoughts and plans, particularly with a trip coming up to Bogotá for the annual international Christian conference.

One evening Mel had a very direct daughter/father chat with me. "Now Dad, please listen carefully to me. Lina's mum will be at the conference, and she will almost certainly want to thank you for looking after Lina. She will probably invite you to a meal with my brothers. If she invites you, you should just go."

Before she got any further, I interrupted. "Mel, I know you mean well, but I didn't expect you to join the matchmakers. I thought I was safe with you! Please let's talk about something else."

Mel however was on a roll and continued, "Seriously, Dad, listen. I have found out quite a lot about this lady and we have had her daughter stay here with us, so we have a pretty good idea of what she is like. She's a very committed Christian. She's a great mum, she's been well-trained in a great church, she's got a great attitude, she likes many of the things you like, she's a confident businesswoman, she's used to speaking to people in public, plus… she is beautiful."

She paused for effect and then said very slowly, "D-a-d, o-p-e-n y-o-u-r e-y-e-s."

At this moment I had a sudden flash of revelation of the truth of Mel's words, and I fell to the ground overwhelmed with joy and gratitude.

Well, no, actually I didn't… but I certainly was touched by my daughter's love for me, and I thought that this was quite a sales pitch for Adriana. She could not have had a better public relations advocate if she had paid for one, which I presumed she hadn't.

Mel, however, was not finished, "One more thing Dad, do you remember when we watched the romantic comedy film Hitch together as a family? When it finished you said the Latina actress in that film, Eva Mendes, was very beautiful and if there was a Christian Eva Mendes out there, she might just have a chance with you."

"Really Mel, I said that?"

"You did, Dad! And Adriana looks just like Eva Mendes."

I was able to personally confirm that assessment just a week or so later. At the end of a conference session in Bogotá, Adriana walked towards me looking as beautiful, and indeed film-star-like, as my daughter had described. It was only our second meeting, but already, I was seeing her in a whole new light.

There were plenty of people milling about, but I was paying more attention to "Lina's mum" than to anyone else. I greeted her with a smile and a light kiss on the cheek. She received this in the natural manner of a trusted friend which I felt she now was, not least because Lina had done such a great job representing her.

After some initial chat with my sons and I, all translated by Lina, she then seemed to be quoting from the script that Mel had prepared me for. "Pastor Wes, you were very kind to Lina in England. I would like to thank you by inviting you and your sons to a meal at my house."

Unfortunately, I couldn't accept the date she had in mind because of my itinerary. Not wanting to miss out on the moment however, I suggested that maybe we could go to a restaurant a little later if that would work. Adriana recalled:

When he suggested a restaurant, I did wonder if it was because he felt it would be safer for him after what my daughter had said about my cooking. But Lina whispered to me and told me to relax. So, we waited for him to finish some meetings. I offered to drive them in my car. When he saw it, he seemed surprised.

My own recollection was one of having a somewhat surreal experience when we reached Adriana's car. For it was the same make, model and colour of my own black Mercedes back home. The only difference was the steering wheel on the opposite side.

I pondered this coincidence as Adriana drove us patiently and safely through the stressful late-evening rush-hour traffic to one of Bogotá's best neighbourhoods, in Usaquén, in the north of the city. It was full of impressive new-world restaurants and old-world charm with its colonial Spanish buildings and cobblestone streets.

When we parked, I waited to walk with Adriana and Lina. I saw that James and Lina's boyfriend, Raul, were walking ahead and chatting, evidently with some amusement. We were not close enough to overhear but they subsequently disclosed that they were saying, "and now it begins."

With hindsight, it certainly felt that way from the moment we stepped into one of Adriana's favourite restaurants. It had a very Mediterranean ambience with displays of hams and cheeses and walls lined with racks of fine wine. As I surveyed the welcoming surroundings and looked directly at the stunning Adriana, who James had carefully seated opposite me, I thought that for sure there were worse ways to spend an evening.

We ordered the food and drinks as naturally as if we were old friends. Adriana was happy to agree to my suggestion that maybe we could share some tapas dishes. Her son, Jose, who also spoke English, joined us to help Lina and Raul with translation, so conversation and laughter flowed freely between us all. Throughout the evening, I felt very at ease with Adriana. It had been a very long time since I felt so content. For her part Adriana recalled:

After all the years of seeing "Pastor Wes" at a distance I really enjoyed just relaxing with him in such an ordinary way and getting to know him. I found that he was very down-to-earth and had a great sense of humour.

Over the busy next few days, we had several pleasant, but brief, informal conversations between conference sessions. When the conference finished, I headed up to the Caribbean coastal resort of Cartagena for a brief holiday with some family and friends.

I didn't get the chance to say goodbye to Adriana, but I didn't want her to think that I had forgotten her. So, I sent a nice box of Belgium chocolates via Lina as a thank you for her "thank you" meal. Adriana said:

I was very happy when Lina said that Pastor Wes had not only sent me chocolates but white chocolates, my favourite. I wouldn't share them with Lina or anyone!

Shortly afterwards Adriana was not only fasting chocolates but all food. Adriana remembers:

Towards the end of the conference, Pastor Emma Claudia, came over for a personal chat with me. She wanted to know whether I was still praying for a husband. I said, "Yes." Then she asked me if I was interested in Pastor Wes. I was a little embarrassed, but I said, "Yes." I shared how I had admired him for some years but now that my daughter had stayed at his home, I was thinking more seriously that there could be possibilities between us.

She smiled and said that it was very important that "You pray to know what can develop between you. I will pray too." She was so kind and supportive.

When the conference ended, I stayed at home for three days and fasted to know God's will for my life. I only drank water, and I read some Scriptures that really spoke to me. I had been waiting a long time for the right husband and I didn't want to make a mistake by just following my own emotions. At the end of the fast, although I didn't know how it could happen or when it would happen, I now felt sure that Pastor Wes was going to be my husband.

Meanwhile up in Cartagena, Adriana's prayers were clearly having an effect. She kept being brought to my attention.

On the first night, I went out for a meal with one of our church's leadership couples, Tim and Clair Holmes-

Clough. Clair, who knew how to conquer big challenges having once rowed across the Atlantic, thought that I should embark on a new adventure myself. She said, "Pastor Wes, did you happen to see Lina's mum? She's beautiful. You should think seriously about meeting up with her."

On the second evening my daughter-in-law, Wilana, took me aside and asked, "Did you see Lina's mum at the conference? I met her and she's lovely. You should think about her."

She also expressed her surprise at having seen me out running on the beach when she, Wes, and the boys had gone out for an early morning walk. She wondered if this new "keep fit" routine was in any way connected with Adriana. I just grinned and said nothing that would further incriminate me.

On the third day, Sarah Plumley, one of the young ladies who was helping to look after my grandkids, said: "I am a bit embarrassed to say this to my pastor, but I believe I saw your future wife at the conference. It's Lina's mum."

These messages were lodged in my mind when we all returned to Bogotá. Most of the group were returning home but, unusually, I was able to stay on for a few more days to have some father-and-son time with Wesley, who was attending a business conference. And that's when a window of opportunity opened for further meetings with Adriana.

Adriana and Lina were our drivers to church that Sunday. The next night, they picked us up to have the long-promised "thank you meal" in her smart apartment in the north of the city.

Wesley, who had a stomach bug, loyally agreed to come with me to support his dad. Although he could not eat much, I certainly enjoyed all three courses, especially the memorably flavoured main dish of salmon teriyaki. Adriana could cook very well after all! *Qué rico!* (Delicious!)

As we relaxed, I noticed that our family Christmas card was still on display. Wesley showed Adriana some pictures of him and his happy family. At this I noticed Adriana's eyes moistening a little. I perceived that such family images stirred something deep inside her.

In this moment, I could feel my previously very well-guarded heart opening in a new way towards Adriana. I now clearly saw not just the capable woman who had first appeared so confidently and elegantly in my office, but also a more vulnerable person who had courageously battled through a lot of pain with a broken family.

The next day she told me more of her life story and her journey as a Christian over an impromptu meal together, with Lina, at a cosy Italian restaurant, La Toscana. But why was she bothering to talk about her life if I was just a passing visitor? And why was she so interested in hearing about my life? Why were we so readily talking about our likes, our setbacks, and hopes? How was it that we were on the same wavelength and so easily laughing together?

Consciously or subconsciously, it seemed that we were trying to get to know each other as quickly as possible in this unexpected, but limited, time together.

We met again for a further meal that same day after Wesley whispered to me, "Dad something is happening here. Don't worry about our time together. Make the most of this time." And so, we maximised our time together in different settings.

One lunch was kindly arranged by Adriana's friend, Pastor Yolanda, who had helped set up our first meeting in my office. I was touched by her love for Adriana and by the way she welcomed me and sat me close to Adriana. She evidently had a very clear vision of a future for us together.

On the last day, as I walked next to Adriana on our way to a coffee shop, I experienced an almost physical sensation that the side of me that had felt so raw and exposed in the wake of Carol's loss, was now once more being covered.

We came even closer together as we posed for a picture before leaving. In that moment, I knew that I was not wrong to imagine that Adriana was also feeling drawn to me.

For she very naturally put her arm lightly around me and tilted her head in slightly. I was a little surprised by this, but I felt no compulsion to protest. She recalled:

At that moment I hadn't planned to reveal how interested I was. But I instinctively put my arm around Wes. I felt that this would be our first picture together.

When I checked the picture, we certainly looked like a very well-established couple. But we were not a couple. We had made no declarations of love or intent to one another. Yet something significant had undoubtedly happened in those few days that both of us clearly recognised.

As we waited to go through airport security, I looked at this smiling and beautiful lady just standing there with such poise and peace. I was reluctant to let her out of my sight and felt subdued by the thought of not knowing how or when we might meet again.

Adriana recalled,

I could see a little sadness in Wes's eyes, but this wasn't the moment to tell him not to worry because I now knew that I was going to be his wife.

CHAPTER 6
TAKING THE PLUNGE

On my return to London, I found it difficult to get Adriana out of my mind. It was just over half a day since I had last seen her, and already I was missing her. I didn't want to make any rash comments or premature commitments, but I did want her to know that she was still very much in my thoughts. So, I sent some pictures from Heathrow Airport showing that I had arrived safely home. Despite the time difference, she didn't take too long to reply. She expressed her pleasure that I was safe and sound.

This had the effect of making me simultaneously elated and disorientated. *Now what? What is going on here? What do I do now? Oh, dear Lord help me!* I felt well out of my comfort zone and far too old for this kind of adolescent "butterflies-in-the-stomach" sensation.

I wanted to have more contact with Adriana, but I was not at all sure whether I was ready, willing, or able to leap into the great unknown and start a relationship with her. I attempted to give myself some wise pastoral counsel:

Pull yourself together man and just logically process everything that has happened. Yes, Adriana is lovely. Yes, you have been very surprised by the sheer joy you felt just being with her. But get real; you are a father of 3 married children, grandfather of 13 and a senior pastor with lots of people and plenty of responsibilities to consider. You don't just go out on a limb and act on a romantic whim at your age and stage of life, especially with someone who lives half a world away and doesn't even speak the same language. Maybe all that has happened in the past few days was just a pleasant and unexpected interlude in your otherwise structured life. Maybe you have just met a really nice friend.

I also considered the unlikely possibility that since Bogotá was 8,660 feet (2,640 metres) above sea level, I had just been suffering some kind of altitude sickness and that any light-headedness would soon wear off back at home. Finally, I got a grip on my swirling thoughts. I decided to have no further contact with Adriana until I had ten days to pray and fast about the future of my life and even, possibly, our lives together.

Back in Colombia, Adriana was in a far more peaceful state than me having already fasted and prayed for guidance and received her answer about the prospect of a relationship with me.

She recalls:

My pastors had told me to just be quiet and say nothing. They said that if this truly was God's will then Pastor Wes would make the contact, and I should just wait to see what would develop. So, as the Bible says, I "waited patiently" in this time, but I also waited expectantly. I checked my phone constantly to see if there were any messages from the English pastor!

My own time of prayer and fasting was not as disciplined or as focussed as Adriana's had been. I went on a similar vegetable fast as the one outlined with the Biblical character Daniel. But my prayers were frequently hijacked by images of the time I had spent with Adriana. I felt they were quite heavenly images.

Five days into my fast, my daughter, Melody, reminded me that it was Valentine's Day. She suggested that I should send a message or even a little present to the lovely Latina who she had earlier recommended to me in such glowing terms. I was obviously feeling some kind of pressure because I was too firm in my response to my well-meaning daughter. "Look Mel," I said, "there's no relationship between us and contacting her today probably wouldn't be a good idea, especially as I am still fasting for guidance."

Having been given such a clear brush-off by me, Mel recalls her surprise when all of fifteen minutes later I told her that I had, in fact, seen the wisdom of her advice and had duly contacted Adriana. I told her I had received a very nice response from Adriana. I showed it to Mel and then I found myself privately and repeatedly picking up my phone to re-read her message.

Mel, having shown commendable forgiveness and understanding recalls:

I realised that my dad was falling in love with Adriana but was having trouble admitting it. I was very amused by how happy he was when he received a reply to his message. He let out a very loud "YESSSS!" and couldn't stop smiling!

My ten days of prayer ended with no immediate clarity about what to do next. Within a week, however, everything quickly fell into place during a brief trip to Israel. I had got up early to see the sunrise over the sparkling Sea of Galilee opposite the Golan Heights. It was hard to imagine that, not so far away, there was so much destruction and death. For, as I surveyed the rolling green hills and the fishing boats bobbing on the softly lapping waters, there was such tranquillity, like nothing had changed much over thousands of years.

With a gentle breeze blowing and the day warming up, I just stood alone at the water's edge and tried to take everything in. I found it very easy to pray. I was surprised at how much I wanted to unburden my heart from both the recent and the distant past. In the silence with no one around, it all started to come out. But after a while I stopped praying, as I gradually felt a great peace enveloping me. It was like a storm of many years was being stilled inside of me, just as had happened on this very sea so long ago.

I had known encounters with God before, but this was different. I didn't hear any audible voice from heaven, but I sensed that the same Jesus who worked so many miracles around Galilee was whispering to me, *"I have watched over you and guided you all through your life and I will watch over you and guide you for the rest of your life. Just listen to me and trust me to lead you in new ways."* I could feel the turmoil of my heart and mind just ebbing away. I now wondered why I had been anxious about so many things. Why had it been so complicated to try and process all that had obviously happened in my heart in Colombia?

I was glad no one was around because I couldn't stop the tears trickling down my face. In those very mellow moments, lasting nearly two hours, I rededicated my life to Christ and surrendered my fears and my future to Him. There and then, I decided that I would leave the past behind me and stop fretting about all the details of how everything would work out from this point on. I resolved to take a step of faith to see if Adriana would be my wife.

On returning home, I called the family together to tell them what I had in my heart to do. When you are younger it's usual to talk to your parents about getting married. When you are older you consult your kids. When I asked them, "What would you think if I got married again?" they were all very supportive. James, who had helped oversee the first restaurant meal with Adriana in Bogotá, just smiled knowingly as if the penny had finally dropped with me. He spoke for them all, "Go for it, Dad. It's time for you to leave home!"

The next step I needed to take was to call Adriana's pastor and spiritual father, Pastor César Castellanos. I knew Adriana would want his blessing and guidance and I did too. We had talked on many occasions and on many subjects, but now I needed to have a very personal conversation with him. I recognised that he was a leader with great wisdom and decisiveness. I therefore knew that there would be no "going back" once I called him and told him my thoughts and intentions. So, with my newfound confidence from my time in Israel, I asked for a FaceTime meeting.

We had a warm initial chat and then I cut to the chase. "Pastor César, you know I really love your church; you have so many special people but there's one member of your flock that I think I love a lot more than the others."

I told him how I had spent some time with Adriana during the recent visit to Bogotá and that I was attracted to her. But, since I didn't really know her, and he had been her pastor for over a decade, I needed him to tell me whether or not he thought that it was right or realistic to start a romantic relationship with her. I recall saying, "In my position, I can't make a mistake. So I would really appreciate your wisdom and advice."

Pastor César listened carefully and was very helpful in his counsel. He was very honouring towards Adriana. He told me that she was highly respected by many in the large MCI church and that she had seen so many positive changes in her life from the moment she became a Christian. She was a true and very faithful disciple and leader, "one of our best," he said. He concluded that if I wanted to pursue a relationship with Adriana, and she was happy, then that was fine by him.

Knowing that he often seemed as well informed as the Israeli Mossad or the CIA, I couldn't resist asking if he happened to know whether Adriana was interested in me. Clearly, he knew that his wife, Pastor Emma Claudia, had, unknown to me, been wisely advising Adriana. However, he just smiled and replied enigmatically, "There were two trees in the Garden of Eden, the Tree of

Knowledge and the Tree of Life. Stick with the tree of life."

As soon as our call ended, and without any additional knowledge of how Adriana might respond, I decided to go in search of the "Tree of Life." I asked Lina to set up a FaceTime meeting with her mum. One way or another this was going to be a defining conversation. Now was the time for me to take the plunge off the high board in order to find out whether I would belly flop or make a smooth landing.

I was both excited and undoubtedly a little nervous as I listened to the ringtones on FaceTime. When I saw Adriana appear on screen, I realised why I had been missing her. She was as beautiful and lovely in her manner as I had remembered from a few weeks back. Of course, I needed to choose my words wisely, not least because Lina was translating everything that I wanted to say. Imagine that!

I began as courteously as I knew. "Adriana, thank you so much for your recent hospitality. I know we thanked you before, but you really looked after us so well. So, I want to thank you again. Thank you for the meals at the restaurant and at your house. Thank you for taking time out to drive me to all my appointments and have some more meals with us. Thank you…"

As I spoke, I was thinking, *"Oh no, this is beginning to sound like a speech at the Oscars… Come on, man… get on with it…"*

I continued, "so… I was just wondering whether all that you did for us was because you are just naturally kind to everybody or (slight pause) because you had any feelings for me."

There I said it… take off… the point of no return.

Adriana was listening carefully and giving nothing away. By now Lina was translating like a robot, as if she didn't know either of us.

Before Adriana could answer I continued, "I would like to know your answer to that question. But it's not fair for you to tell me before I tell you what I am thinking because I'm the one calling you.

"So, I need to be vulnerable with you and I don't want you to feel bad if I have got the signals wrong because I am a big boy and can deal with that. But what I want you to know, Adriana, is that while I was in Colombia, something special happened in my heart towards you. In fact, I loved every moment I was with you, and I haven't stopped thinking about you ever since."

At this point, I knew I had to wrap up my little speech with an impressive declaration of my love. But all I could think at that moment were of the words of my sons when they asked their future wives to marry them. They had each used a quote from the film *Dumb and Dumber* starring Jim Carrey. And, so, it came to pass that in this key moment of unfolding destiny I found myself saying, "Adriana, I want to tell you that I really like you a lot."

Yes, I know that as a man of words I should have come up with something far more eloquent and poetic than a corny line from a Hollywood movie. But I hadn't prepared a speech and that's what came out. Anyway, it looked like it was beginning to get through to Adriana.

Finally, I told her, "I have spoken to my family about my feelings for you. I have talked to your pastor to explain how I feel and so now, I need to know how you feel. Would you be interested in starting a romantic relationship with me?"

Oh yes, thank you, Lord… finally I got there…

As Lina faithfully translated everything into Spanish, I watched and waited expectantly for her Mum's reaction. Then I saw a big smile appear on Adriana's face which needed no interpreter. Without any hesitation Adriana said just one word in Spanish that even I understood: "Si."

Yes! She said yes! She said YES! This time I really was feeling overwhelmed with joy and gratitude. Adriana just sat there smiling and waited for me to speak.

"Well, Adriana, I don't quite know what I was expecting but I wasn't expecting such a clear response straight away. "Si?" Is that it? I don't know whether to laugh, kiss the computer screen, or shout a Hallelujah."

"Do it all," she said.

Later, Adriana explained why she was so quick in her response:

I was very pleased when Lina told me that Pastor Wes wanted a personal talk with me. I threw my arms up in the air in excitement because I guessed what it would be about. Lina laughed.

Although I had believed he would be my husband I imagined that it might take a year or so for anything to happen. I was a bit surprised when he called so soon.

When he spoke, I thought, 'Wow, this guy is really sincere and romantic. He is also very courageous and determined.' I really admired that. I wanted someone who would be decisive and bold in his actions. I wanted someone who would have the faith to overcome any obstacles, like language or distance, to win me. I always liked the movies where the prince arrives for his princess.

I felt that God had already shown me that when my Prince called on me, I should say "yes" straight away so that's exactly what I did. I didn't want to play any games with him but just give him a sincere reply.

In that moment, I felt very happy but also very thankful to God for His faithfulness. I waited for many years for the right man to come at the right moment for the fulfilment of God's promise. And now, suddenly, here he was.

Over the next few weeks there were many more FaceTime conversations, and our daily routines underwent a major change. Adriana and I juggled the six-hour time difference and our various responsibilities to speak twice a day and gaze at each other on a computer screen while Lina struggled valiantly to stay awake.

Nevertheless, she patiently endured conversations such as when Adriana mentioned the word "Jubilee," which signifies a Biblical time of celebration and new beginnings. I thought this idea of Jubilee was relevant for us, as it involves a whole year of favour and freedom, a complete reset of what had gone before.

At one point in the conversation, and not just because I agreed with what she was saying, I asked Adriana to repeat the word "Jubilee" several times in English. After the fourth or fifth attempt Adriana looked confused and asked why she needed to keep repeating this word. What was she doing wrong?

"No, you are saying it fine," I replied with a smile. "I just love how you shape your lips when you say 'Jubilee'." (Go on, try it, dear reader!)

Lina also acted as a content supervisor. On one occasion when she clearly felt Adriana was being too warm in her words to me, she intervened like a dutiful parent with an over-exuberant child, to say, "Enough, Mami!"

To get some time alone with each other, Adriana and I learnt to prepare for our talks with questions and comments which we had each diligently researched; Adriana in English and me in Spanish. It was hard work constantly rehearsing how to be spontaneous in another language. Overall, we did surprisingly well in the development of our communication, but FaceTime talks had their limitations. We wanted to get together as soon as possible and develop our relationship informally before too many people discovered what was unfolding.

We both thought that Miami, known as the melting pot of many cultures, would be a neutral and romantic location for our next date. It was not completely a midway point, but we would both feel at home in an English and Spanish speaking city.

We agreed to meet up on a day that was all about new beginnings.

CHAPTER 7
MEETING UP IN MIAMI

I love the excitement of Easter Sundays. Ever since I was a child our church has always enthusiastically celebrated Christ's resurrection and the hope of new life.

I recall the passion of large congregations singing classic hymns like Charles Wesley's, "Christ the Lord is Risen Today" and the thundering, "Up from the grave He arose with a mighty triumph over His foes."[i]

Now half a century later, on Easter Sunday March 27, 2016, my steps quickened in anticipation of another powerful morning as I approached the Theatre Royal, Windsor, opposite Windsor Castle, where King's Church International held their public services.

I was not disappointed. All three levels were packed with people that represented many nationalities and age groups. Everybody was clearly happy to be there, and the singing of old favourites and new songs was inspiring.

People listened attentively as I preached from a verse in Luke 24:5-6, "Why do you look for the living among the dead? He is not here, He has risen."

In my message I said: "The Easter story tells us that the awful darkness of Good Friday was followed by the bright new dawn of Easter Sunday.

"The foundational claim of Christianity is that Jesus certainly was dead but that He didn't stay dead. And today, 2000 years on, despite the best efforts of scoffers and sceptics, the Christian church still confidently proclaims that truth.

"The Easter story is the greatest turnaround story in history, and it points to how your life can turn around too."

I felt empowered as I spoke but, in truth, it took a lot of discipline to concentrate. In the back of my mind, I was very much aware of how my own life was about to turn around that very day as I anticipated meeting with Adriana.

As soon as the service finished, I went backstage to greet my children and grandchildren, had a quick change of clothes, and then slipped out a side door to a waiting car.

My ever-faithful friend, Terry Beasley, now seeing the fruit of his own subtle matchmaking manoeuvres the previous summer, drove me to Heathrow Airport, with Margaret, who had been like a big sister to me from childhood. They seemed almost as excited as I was. Both were clearly enjoying their part of my somewhat clandestine travel plans. I made it to the gate just in time for the British Airways flight to Miami.

I eagerly anticipated the moment of arrival in the hazy heat of Florida where I would have my first rendezvous with Adriana since she had agreed to start a romantic relationship with me. As much as I had enjoyed the twice-daily FaceTime meetings with Adriana, it hopefully would be a very different experience to have a much closer face-to-face.

I had nearly nine hours to catch up on some sleep and to dream of how we would greet one another. Should I be the understated English gentleman and walk slowly and self-confidently towards her with an enticing smile? Perhaps I could wear my Panama hat and gently lift it off my head as an old-fashioned sign of respect? Or, perhaps, I should just go all out to destroy any possible stuffy British stereotypes from the start? Maybe I should just run towards her, sweep her up in my arms and kiss her until she felt overcome with bliss and ecstasy?... Or maybe not.

What if she had plans of her own? What if she rushed to embrace me wildly? What if the mere sight of me unleashed some primal Latina passions in Adriana? That could be embarrassing… And highly unlikely!

Obviously, I had seen a few too many rom-coms like *Maid in Manhattan* where Latina Jennifer Lopez and an American politician fall in love. But I need not have worried. For, at the very moment the automatic doors opened in the arrivals hall, and I walked through with great expectations, Adriana was nowhere to be seen. She truly was a Latina, and a Colombian Latina at that, which meant she had just popped over to the coffee shop after a long wait.

When she came to meet me a few minutes later, I was looking the other way. She tapped me on the shoulder and caught me off guard in an airport full of strangers. I jumped back, startled.

Adriana couldn't help laughing and so did plenty of other people later, when they saw Lina's very funny video recording of the intended drama of this special moment. Once I realised that it was Adriana who was trying to get my attention, I laughed too.

I quickly evaluated her beautiful face and figure and an obviously new floral dress. Her makeup was immaculate. Her hair once again was styled to perfection. She could not have looked more elegant. Wow, wow and more wow! So here we go…

I recovered my composure to lean in and give her a long-awaited kiss. But as I did so she gently tilted her head to merely receive an innocent peck on the cheek. I tried to hide my surprise as we walked together with Lina to the car hire centre. Adriana was friendly enough. The atmosphere however, if not the climate, was a few degrees cooler than I had expected. "Well," I thought, "that certainly didn't go the way I planned it."

On the way to the homes of friends, I soon discovered what was going on in the mind of the lovely Colombiana. Through Lina, our ever-valiant interpreter, Adriana explained that she wanted our relationship to develop in the stages advised by her church. This was news to me since we hadn't discussed it in any of our conversations.

Pastor Johanna Castellanos Proença, who had faithfully mentored Adriana over many years, had written a book designed to help couples prepare to build long-lasting marriages by progressing through various stages. This involved first becoming special friends, then boyfriend and girlfriend, fiancés, and finally, if all went well, husband and wife, while presumably remaining good friends. My daughter and others in our church had told me that this was a very helpful book. Unfortunately, it had not been on top of my reading list nor even on my list. So, I was ignorant about what state of grace I was in at that moment.

Adriana presumed that, as a pastor with years of association with her church, I knew all about these widely practised dating protocols. So, I needed to come clean and confess to her that I hadn't read the book. Adriana seemed surprised but clarified that, at this moment in time, we were at the "special friends" stage in what seemed to me a kind of old-world chaperone arrangement. This meant apparently that while we were allowed the great concession of holding hands, we could not even kiss until we had decided to commit to developing the relationship.

I tried to calmly process this unexpected conversation as I drove us, on the right side of the road, or for the British "wrong side" of the road, with my body clock registering about 3am. I considered my thoughts and words carefully. I have never been a fan of legalistic religious rules, but I could see why practical guidelines had real value. Certainly, I had witnessed how there were many strong marriages in Adriana's church which ministered amidst an epidemic of broken homes.

Adriana wanted to know whether I was "OK" to

follow "the process." I thought she was a bit nervous, so I tried to inject some ironic British humour into the conversation. "So let me get this clear, I have spoken to my family. I have spoken to your pastor to tell him of my love for you. I have just flown across an ocean to see you and now I don't even get a kiss."

Adriana didn't seem to know what to make of my cross-cultural attempt at wit, so I thought it best to reassure her that I was fine to let events unfold. Once we had arrived at our destination, I decided to go ahead anyway and give her some diamond earrings that Mel advised me to buy for my future girlfriend/special friend/future wife or whatever she was at that moment. Adriana seemed very pleased with this. She recalled:

I was really looking forward to meeting my "special friend" and I was a little anxious that we had this misunderstanding right at the start. But when he gave me this lovely present, I felt more relaxed because to me this was a sign that he was already very committed in his heart towards me.

I, too, was somewhat relieved to see some restoration of the easy rapport that I had known with Adriana previously. I was also reassured that my hosts, Richard Harding from Newcastle, UK, and his wife Manuela Castellanos from Bogotá, were a living example of the love that could blossom in an Anglo/Colombian relationship.

After a relaxing supper at their home, Adriana left me with a warm, but passion-free goodbye to stay with Lina at the home of other pastors from the Miami branch of Pastor César's church. Finally, at around 11 p.m., or 5 a.m. of the next day British time, I made it to my room and fell into a deep and contented sleep after the longest Easter Sunday that I could remember.

I woke up to a beautiful Florida spring morning happy with life and Adriana. I was impressed that she placed such importance on building a strong foundation for our relationship. I reflected that it was probably wise to take things steadily and slowly. Well, that certainly seemed a good idea at the time, but during the day events started to accelerate.

On Easter Monday, we drove to an idyllic palm tree-fringed beach in Fort Lauderdale. And there, suddenly and naturally, Adriana slipped her soft hand into mine for the first time. I couldn't believe how pleasant this innocent development was. At one point a little later, when Adriana moved closer towards me, I sensed that she wanted to kiss me. I smiled with some satisfaction and told her mischievously just to stay with the process.

I also wondered what our family would think if they could see us strolling together barefoot through the warm waters of a Florida beach. I imagined with some amusement that many church family and friends would have been amazed to see their pastor in such a paradise with this beautiful lady just 24 hours after preaching in Windsor. They would never have expected this. As much as I was relishing every moment, I was also struggling to believe this was happening.

Adriana also seemed happy to be with her new "special friend." She recounted:

I was very excited to finally hold hands and walk like a

couple. This was the moment when Pastor Wes became Wes, my romantic boyfriend and the man of my dreams. I hoped he was not too discouraged after our chat the night before, so I walked very close to him and squeezed his hand a lot. Actually, I did want to kiss him as everything was so romantic. But of course, Lina was always with us and translating for us so I thought, 'Ok, then, let's follow the plan.'

For my part, I didn't think our current relationship status would last long whatever the book said. Just a few hours later my instincts proved correct when everything went into overdrive.

That evening we went for what I had thought would be a quiet meal at the home of Pastors William and Liliana Raad, sister of Pastor Emma Claudia Castellanos. We were exchanging some pleasant initial greetings when Pastors César and Emma Claudia walked in. I had no idea that they were coming. We were both so pleased to see them.

From the moment of their arrival it was like being in two Porsche cars that went from 0-60mph in less than three seconds. From the start it was clear that they were focussed on helping us lay a strong foundation for our relationship. Pastor Emma Claudia was soon in a huddle with Adriana and seemed excited to get to the subject at hand as soon as we all sat together by a poolside table.

Naturally, I sat next to Adriana who was wearing another beautiful, full-length, new dress patterned with red roses. The atmosphere was very relaxed, and the steaks and spicy Colombian salads were excellent. The highlight of this evening, however, was a pastoral and prophetic conversation that I will never forget.

MEETING UP IN MIAMI

The pastors asked us to recount the story of how we met and how our relationship was developing. I told them about our unexpected chat on the ride from the airport. Adriana and I both said that it was probably a good idea to take a bit of time to slowly get to know each other without feeling any pressure.

Pastor Emma Claudia smiled and then gently pointed out that the book had really been aimed at generations somewhat younger than us. *"Amen to that,"* I thought. She commended Adriana for being so careful to obey good advice. However, she thought that our current "special friends" status didn't have to last too long. She said that she and her husband had seen many indications that our relationship was a gift from God. She also reminded Adriana how, previously, she had shared that one day she, like Rebekah in the Old Testament, would leave her home at the right moment when her "Isaac" arrived. "Well," said Pastor Emma Claudia, "now that moment has arrived, and your 'Isaac' is Pastor Wes."

Pastor César said that he thought that it was not a coincidence that it was on Easter Sunday when we had met up. He could see that God had brought me to a place where I was ready for a new beginning. He also thought that it was significant that my daughter, Melody, and my family were so positive about our relationship. They felt that it was remarkable how everything had worked out for Lina to stay with us at my home.

Pastor César told me, "We get to know God the Father because of the way Jesus represented him. Lina introduced you to the mother. You could see her character through Lina."

Pastor César went on to say how he and everyone in the leadership in Bogotá had the highest respect for Adriana - for her character, her faithfulness, her family, and her love for God. Then he came right out with it and gently told Adriana, "I don't see you in Colombia anymore. You should leave your home country and go to the UK to be with Pastor Wes. You will be like Ruth who went with Naomi. From now on you will see an acceleration in everything, including learning English."

Pastor César recalled how I had first gone to Colombia with a broken heart. He then turned to me and said, "Pastor Wes, God brought you to Bogotá to heal your heart and now that it is healed, it is through Bogotá that you have now found a wife."

Such was the power of Pastor César's words that it felt like he had married us there and then. So then, no more boyfriend and girlfriend! We were going through the stages of the process almost as fast as I was learning what they were. Adriana was taking it all in very quietly. I wondered what she was feeling about such declarations for our future. I gave her hand a quick squeeze.

Adriana responded by saying that at the start of our friendship I had shared a scripture with her which I felt applied to our future together. She said that she had anticipated that it might be some romantic verse from the Song of Solomon like she had long ago put in her dream book. Instead, she was surprised to hear me quote from the words of Jesus in Matthew 11:28-30 which seemed somewhat out of context with the elation we were both feeling:

> *"Come to me, all you who are weary and burdened, and I will give you rest. Take my yoke upon you and learn from me, for I am gentle and humble in heart, and you will find rest for your souls. For my yoke is easy and my burden is light."*

Adriana recalled:

Wes said that with all the changes and challenges our relationship may involve we should never become stressed. God wanted us to stay in an attitude of having rest in our souls. If we were to be yoked together then we should both be confident that we would always experience an ease and lightness of spirit if we stayed close to the Lord and we learned from Him to be humble and gentle with each other.

At first, I wondered why he had quoted verses about being burdened and weary, but I began to see how relevant they were. They gave me a strong sense of security as we were taking some very big steps into the unknown.

Our turbocharged evening ended with Pastor César praying a moving prayer thanking God for His loving direction over our lives.

Before we said goodbye to everyone, Adriana and I had a few minutes alone. We sat on a sofa by the pool holding hands like a couple of young kids, smiling at each other, but unable to say much without a translator. We still hadn't even kissed, and we could speak no more than a few phrases to each other, but I too now felt sure that much sooner, rather than later, Adriana would be my wife.

. . .

Adriana recalled:

I felt like I was experiencing a miracle. That evening was like discovering a treasure that I had always been looking for. Now the road was clear for my dream marriage. I was so excited to see what would happen next.

CHAPTER 8
LADY IN THE DREAM

The morning after the game-changing night before I woke up early and wondered if I had been imagining everything that had happened. Reality soon kicked in as I tried to process the many new developments which were unfolding far more rapidly than I had expected.

Before doing anything else, I wanted to quietly focus on my morning time of prayer and Bible reading, a life-long habit that had been an anchor for me in many different seasons of life. As I was praying in these happy but fast-moving circumstances, the thought came to me that I should call my long-time friends Dr Michael ('Pete') and Linda Peters from St. Louis.

Pete and Linda were driving when I reached them to announce that I had some news for them. "Who's having a baby now?" Pete immediately asked, laughing, having received many calls from me about more pregnancies in the family.

"No, it's not that!" I replied.

Before I could say any more Linda cut in, "You're getting married!"

Neither Pete nor I had any idea how she so quickly came to this conclusion. We both went quiet.

I answered by saying that getting married was indeed what I was planning to do. As calmly and concisely as I could, I launched into telling them about my meetings with Adriana and how everything had accelerated. I could hear the shock in Pete's voice as he said, "Hold on a minute, I really need to pull over." Having parked off the highway he said, "I thought I was going to crash my truck when I realised that you weren't joking."

Linda meanwhile didn't seem at all surprised at what she was hearing. She reminded me of the dream that she had shared with me some years before of me marrying a dark-haired lady. "Look Wes, I might have got this wrong, but could you send me a picture of Adriana and then call us back?"

I sent the picture and called again. Linda answered. I could hear that she was emotional and struggling to speak. Then she said quietly, "Wes, Adriana is the lady I saw so clearly in the dream."

I didn't know what to say. I felt my own eyes moistening. This was quite a confirmation that I was moving in the right direction. Gathering myself, I asked if it was possible for them, at such short notice, to fly down and meet us both. They said they could come in a few days for 24 hours. I said I would delay my flight home to see them.

That agreed, I turned my attention to meeting up with Adriana once more in the home of Pastors Richard and Manuela. They were clearly happy to be part of the love story that was unfolding before their eyes, but they were very prudent in what they said to me and diplomatically disappeared when Adriana and Lina arrived. I politely suggested to Lina that she, too, might like to help them out in the kitchen. She took the hint.

Adriana looked at me with some amusement as our trusted interpreter left us to our own devices. I used some basic sign language which involved my forefinger pointing to my pouted lips and a few words of imperfect Spanish. Adriana began to giggle. I could see that I had successfully communicated that now would be a good moment to progress from the special friends stage to being boyfriend and girlfriend. This was the drum roll moment.

And so, at 12.32 p.m. on Tuesday, March 29, 2016, (we British always know the time) I made my move. I leaned over to the flawlessly beautiful face of Adriana, and we kissed softly and rapturously. I am happy to disclose that it was certainly worth the wait!

"Thank God," I thought, *"at last, no more tilted head and a miserly peck on the cheek that had so taken me by surprise on my arrival at the airport."*

But then, in my moment of contented triumph, Adriana pulled back. She looked at me expressionless. I wondered what was happening. I thought, *"I know it has been a long time but surely, I haven't forgotten how to kiss. I can't be that bad."*

Then I saw that she was trying to suppress a smile.

She looked me straight in the eye, puckered her lips and said slowly and deliberately, "J-u-b-i-l-e-e." We both laughed and I got an early insight into the mischievous humour of my new girlfriend and of her elephant-like memory.

When Lina came back into the room, I saw that she was trying to process that her mother and the UK pastor were sitting much closer together than when she had left. Fortunately, she didn't notice Adriana quickly removing some of her lipstick from my face. Later, Lina recalled:

It was funny to see my mature Mum in the shy, girlfriend stage and smiling like an excited teenager. Pastor Wes was grinning like he had just won a gold medal at the Olympics. I was very happy for them.

For the next few days Lina was our chaperone as we three musketeers headed to Orlando for a short break in the city of theme parks. As we drove up the interstate and shared more of our life stories, it felt like we were a long-established family unit. I am sure it looked like that as we visited various restaurants and shops.

It was the simple things which signalled that big changes were happening in my life, both internally and externally. Once, when we went to a giant Walmart store, I was struck by how much I was enjoying simply pushing a trolley along beside Adriana and selecting some food together. I remembered how out of sorts I had often felt when I went alone to the supermarket where couples often shopped casually and happily together. Now even in doing simple tasks, I felt that part of me was being put back together. It was odd to feel as though my heart was receiving healing in the aisles of a superstore, but that's exactly what was happening. I loved Adriana's company and lightness of spirit.

I experienced that same sense of wellbeing when we shared a simple meal together at the apartment that Mel had organised for us. It was more than just relaxing together. It was like I had come home, and normal order had been restored.

It felt very natural to get up early and prepare breakfast for Adriana and Lina, though I wondered what was taking them so long to surface from their room and why it was so noisy with a cacophony of hairdryers, showers, and praise music all competing.

For me all this was a baptism into adjusting to a different culture. I began to learn to be more "tranquilo" about time and to let each day unfold at its own pace. We enjoyed relaxing by the pool, going for walks, and embracing one another - as and when the watchful "Mother Superior" Lina permitted.

Not everything was quite so easy going however, as I discovered when we stopped for a game of crazy golf. Adriana clearly wanted to beat me at all costs, and I was happy not to be beaten. I was highly amused as I witnessed her frustration when she hit some of her shots clean out of the park and mine went obediently, and sometimes by a total fluke, into the holes.

As my lead mounted up, Adriana tried various devious tactics to put me off. Finally, and to my embarrassment with other people around, she started kissing me as I attempted my shots. We abandoned the game, with it abundantly obvious from such juvenile and carefree behaviour, that we were madly in love with each other.

So yet again, we approached another "What now?" moment. Surely at our stage of life, and with all that had happened in the remarkable development of our relationship, there was no point in going through a prolonged intercontinental courtship. Since we both clearly felt that our future was together, I waited for the opportunity to share what was in my heart. This came on a sunny afternoon in a Chinese restaurant overlooking a lake in Disney's Epcot Centre.

During our meal, I told Adriana how much I was enjoying our time together but that I needed her input on a dilemma that I was trying to resolve in my mind. I summarised how I saw our current situation by saying:

"If you were to move to England, I would first have to inquire if it is possible to get a visa for you. The best visa is probably a spouse visa but there is no point in me applying for a spouse visa unless I know for sure that you would become my wife. But you wouldn't become my wife unless I asked you to marry me, which I am not quite ready to do at this moment until I can be sure what the visa situation is. So, this is what's known as a Catch 22 situation."

At this point Lina was struggling to keep up with the translation. Adriana was concentrating hard to try and understand my logic and to figure out where all this was going. I pressed on to try to clarify, "Adriana at some point in the not-too-distant future I would love to marry you, and I will ask you with an official proposal. But unofficially, I would like to know today if you will marry me when I officially ask you."

At this Adriana smiled and said, "Unofficially, I accept your unofficial proposal." And then her tears started flowing. Adriana recalled:

I couldn't believe what I was hearing and that this was happening so quickly. I had imagined that we might go out together for another year or so. But when I heard him speak these words I was overjoyed. I couldn't stop crying. I was so happy as I knew I really loved Wes, and I was confident that he really loved me.

Our translator, my dear future stepdaughter, was also crying because she had mixed emotions about the progression of our relationship. Lina said:

I was in shock at what I was translating. I felt very emotional for my Mum and also for myself. This was what she had always wanted and prayed for. I could see that what was happening between her and Pastor Wes was very real. I remembered that I had prayed that my Mum would get married before me so I could marry Raul and not feel bad that I would leave my Mum alone. I put it in my dream book that she could marry this year.

Although I felt happy for my Mum, at the same time, I felt quite sad. I was confused because I was so dependent on my Mum and so close to her. I was trying to be relaxed about it all, but I wondered how my life was going to change and how everything would work out.

With two crying ladies at the table, I was now even more mindful that our proposed marriage would require a lot of love and wisdom in a time of transition for our families as well as us.

Once all tears were dried however, the three of us walked happily around the various national exhibitions in the park, stopping to get some pictures in the area representing the United Kingdom, hopefully soon to be the home of Adriana.

Once we returned to Miami, Adriana and I headed out to the airport to pick up Pete and Linda. It was a very special moment introducing old friends to a new friend, especially one that Linda had already clearly seen in a dream many years before. Linda, who speaks Spanish, immediately hit it off with Adriana. They were soon chatting rapidly together. Pete and I pulled faces to each other as we unsuccessfully tried to understand them.

As I recall, Pete, at regular intervals which seemed appropriate to him, kept randomly inserting phrases like "Hola" (Hello), "¿Cómo estás?" (How are you?), "Muy bien" (very good), "Si" (yes) and "Gracias" (thank you). This appeared to be the only Spanish he knew. I felt fluent in comparison, although that was nothing to boast about!

Pete and Linda took us out for a surprise celebration meal. They told us how they had both been immediately struck by how much of a natural couple we looked when we had walked hand-in-hand towards them at the airport. I was very pleased to see how happy Adriana was at being adopted so warmly by veteran friends who were like family.

The next day at our request we got together with them and Pastors César and Emma Claudia to receive whatever advice they each wished to give us. Both couples could not have been more encouraging as they lovingly talked and prayed with us.

Pastor César said he was impressed that my whole family was very supportive of our relationship and remarked, "This is proof that God is in this relationship." He said that despite the blessings of my children and grandchildren, there was a void in me at not having someone to share life with. Finding Adriana as my future wife would bring "renewal of strength and love."

Pastor Emma Claudia said that Adriana was "a woman of prayer," who had committed herself fully to God and who had waited for God to give her the right husband. She told her to be confident of a warm welcome in Great Britain, "Just be yourself. The Lord is going to help you in everything."

Pete, who had been with our family through many difficult moments, was emotional as he told us that an old chapter had closed and now God was making "all things new." He didn't think that events were moving too fast and commented:

"When you meet someone that matches your soul, it's as though you've always known each other. It's like a new old friend, rather than starting over. I think that God shapes our souls, and then we look for the person it matches with. And when you find that person, some people say it goes fast, but it only seems that way to us."

He continued, "It's been a lot of years for both of you to come to this moment. But when God brings the pieces of our lives together, we just need to catch up."

To help our friends and churches catch up, we recorded some video messages and shots for the moment when we would announce our romance. And then we all posed for so many photos that it seemed like a wedding rehearsal. Adriana reflected feeling *"so happy to know that we would soon share the news of our amazing dream romance."*

In all the excitement, after I had reluctantly parted from my dream lady, Adriana somehow missed her plane to Colombia. This unscheduled change of plans, however, turned out to be a great blessing.

Pastor Liliana, who was like a sister to Adriana, immediately saw the possibilities of some extra time in Miami. "No problem, Adriana; now we have plenty of time to go together to choose the place for you to get married and to find your wedding dress."

Adriana recalled:

Instead of becoming stressed, Pastor Liliana really helped me to stay rested like Wes had said with the Scripture that he gave me. So, like two excited teenagers, we went to my favourite place to look at wedding dresses. I tried on five or six dresses which were all lovely, but I wasn't sure. So even though it was a practical detail, I prayed for the Holy Spirit's help.

Then the sales lady told us they had just received a new collection from Italy which was not yet on display. She said she had one dress that she thought could work for me.

At that moment, thank God, I had lost some weight because I had exercised every morning in the park outside my apartment. All the time I was sweating, I had been visualising this moment when I would choose the best wedding dress.

The dress that I was presented with was so elegant in a romantic and elegant style. It was a sleeveless body length satin dress. It was covered with hand embroidered flowers in lace all the way to the neck and with a half open back. It had a tightly fitted body and a sweeping train. I loved every detail. It was so beautiful. I was absolutely blown away when I tried it on. It was very heavy, but it fitted me perfectly.

Pastor Liliana, the sales lady and some other shoppers all gathered round, and all said "Wow." So did Lina when we sent some pictures.

I knew this dress was more than I had dreamed of. I couldn't wait to see Wes's reaction when I walked down the aisle to be his princess bride. But at that moment I wasn't sure I wanted to see his face as I had to call him and tell him the price. He seemed a bit quiet at first but then he said, "Enjoy, and go ahead." Pastor Liliana and I hugged each other.

Adriana's call certainly concentrated my mind not just on funding the wedding dress of her dreams but also on the need for sufficient finances for every part of our very unexpected and unbudgeted future journey. However, I didn't intend for any anxiety to creep in and to rob us of our joy. Over the years I had learned from personal experience the truth that, *"Where God guides, He provides."* I felt sure that God would help us in every way.

With renewed faith that everything would work out, I eagerly focussed on planning the next stage of our ever more rapidly accelerating love story.

CHAPTER 9
ENGAGED IN CARTAGENA

Adriana did not yet know it, but my goal was to officially ask her to marry me in the tropical city of Cartagena, Colombia, which I had recently visited. I could not imagine a more romantic place to get engaged. I planned to take her there just four weeks after saying our goodbyes in Miami. Before that, however, a lot needed to be done quickly to make our dreams a reality.

Within hours after returning to London I was back in the air for a second night on another long-haul trip as I needed to honour various ministry commitments with King's Church International in South Africa.

My arrival in the Western Cape gave me the opportunity to catch up with my daughter, Mel, and Drikus who had been covering some Easter events for me in Robertson during my absence. Mel was both amused and amazed as I updated her on how fast everything had moved on since we had last met two weeks before.

By the next day, despite all the demands on her as a mother of five young children, she had figured out a list of what I needed to do while we were together. Somehow, she had found "a friend of a friend" who could source me a beautiful South African diamond ring. I felt completely out of my depth when it came to choosing, but Mel kindly "held my hand" as I figured out what to put on Adriana's hand. With that important matter resolved, I did my best to focus on my mission of training leaders while juggling twice daily FaceTime calls to Adriana on the other side of the world.

To avoid distractions, I waited until the end of the trip to let the Robertson leadership team and other friends in on the new developments that were unfolding in my life. One by one they shared how pleased they were for me and how they had been praying that I would find a very special wife. I hadn't realised that I had been such a hot topic of prayer, but I was touched by their happiness for me.

On my return to the UK, I prepared to tell our church family about my unexpected journey of love. It was a big deal for me to get the timing and announcement right since so many individuals, couples and families had been close to me for so many years. We had walked together through *"many dangers, toils and snares"*[i] as John Newton put it. I wanted everybody to know first-hand from me how this new example of "Amazing Grace" had come about and what was being planned. So, on 1 May 2016, just five weeks after the Easter Sunday service when I had quietly slipped out for a flight to Miami, I was back at the Theatre Royal, Windsor ready to proclaim some "very good news."

The title of my message was *"How God can Amaze You."* I took as my text a verse from Genesis 45:26 which contains just three words. It says simply, "Jacob was stunned."

I said: "This is one of the shortest verses in the Bible, but it has relevance for us today. That little sentence sums up one big story of recovery and restoration. It speaks powerfully of how God's faithfulness and plans can leave you completely amazed."

I told how Jacob, grandson of Abraham, son of Isaac and widowed husband of the beautiful Rachel, had discovered that his favourite son Joseph had been killed. Or so, he was led to believe. I said:

"For years Jacob struggled to get over the sadness in his life. But in one unexpected moment Jacob suddenly realised that all along God had been watching over him. As Romans 8:28 puts it, 'In all things,' God had been working for his good.

"For when Jacob's sons, returned from a trip to Egypt, they had some startling and amazing news. The powerful ruler of Egypt who controlled the food supply for millions, was none other than Jacob's long-lost son Joseph.

"Joseph wasn't dead, and Jacob wasn't finished. A whole new season of life and joy and discovery was at hand. No wonder the Bible says that 'Jacob was stunned; he did not believe them.'"[1]

---
1. Genesis 45:26

I went on to share how God can stun us all in many ways. "God can stun us with how he can intervene in nations and in churches. God can stun us with how he can intervene in families and individual lives."

Then, feeling uncharacteristically nervous, I started to make the link with how this applied to my own life.

"For sure, like Jacob, I have been stunned over the years at the positive developments in my own life and family.

"Well, today, I want to tell you of a further and more recent development that I never saw coming which has absolutely amazed me. And I think you may also be stunned when you hear what I am about to share."

I paused slightly so that I would get my next words out with clarity and composure.

"So, dear church family, I hope you are sitting comfortably… for I am very pleased to tell you that I am soon to become a married man again."

The whole place suddenly went very quiet. It was clear that the good and faithful people of King's Church International were struggling to believe what they had just heard. Some assumed I was joking and were waiting for the punchline. Others whispered to the person next to them to confirm that what I had said was what they thought they had heard. Mostly everyone just looked at me. I just stood there smiling to let the message sink in which it quickly did.

A few moments later, that distinguished Royal Theatre erupted with a level of enthusiasm not always witnessed in British churches, especially in "traditional Windsor." People were on their feet, clapping, cheering and whistling. I had imagined that people would be pleased but I did not expect such an explosion of joy.

My pre-arranged Facebook post went live as I spoke. Some of the younger people were pointing to it on their phones. Word went around "It must be true it's on Facebook!"… which I thought was an interesting commentary of the faith they had in social media rather than the words of their long-time pastor standing in front of them.

There was further celebration as I told the story of our romance. Then I had some fun and asked if they were at all interested in wanting to see some videos and pictures of Adriana and of both of us together. When they duly appeared, it was clear that, like Jacob, many were stunned, some no doubt feeling that God had shown great grace to me as they saw the images of my beautiful prospective bride.

Adriana was watching all this out of sight with great interest over the internet even though it was very early morning in Bogotá.

Adriana recalled:

I was so excited observing everything with Lina from in my apartment. I felt very reassured at the positive response from people who would soon be my new church family. I could see that these British Christians were not as reserved as I had imagined them to be. They were reacting like passionate Colombians. I was very moved also to see how much they loved Wes.

Next, it was my turn to follow events over the internet as, a few hours later, Pastor César announced our news in Adriana's huge home church in Bogotá and interviewed her about our romance. I, too, was happy to see Adriana's joy and composure and the enthusiastic response of so many people to our story of hope.

The rest of that still well-remembered day was a full day of greetings and celebrations before saying goodbyes again to the family. That evening, with the engagement ring in my pocket, I headed back to Heathrow to board yet another plane to Colombia ready to propose to Adriana.

By now, I was getting used to the Avianca flight number: AV 121. It reminded me of Psalm 121 which had become very special to our family as it speaks of how the Lord watches over our "coming and going both now and forevermore."[2]

Adriana, together with Lina and boyfriend Raul, met me in the early hours of the morning in Bogotá. A few hours later, joined by her son, Jose, we flew together to Cartagena for what proved to be my most memorable visit to date.

Adriana recounts:

I had been many times before with my children and church friends and always enjoyed the wonderful food, the atmosphere, and the beautiful weather that is the same all year round. But I always wished that I could be there, in such a romantic place, with the man of my dreams.

For me too, like countless other visitors, poets, artists and writers, I had become increasingly enchanted by the Old Town, with its maze of classically designed squares, spectacular churches and regal colonial buildings.

---

2. Psalm 121:8

By day it was like exploring a lavish film set featuring palm trees, vividly dressed street vendors, restaurants, and cafés for every taste.

By night, it was magical to safely wander the narrow cobblestone streets with its many overhanging balconies full of multi-coloured exotic flowers. Everything was illuminated by antique lanterns which gave off a relaxing yellow glow and transformed the pastel shades of 400-year-old houses. And, to cap it all, there was nearly always a light sea breeze to cool you enough to eat outside in perfect conditions. And that's what we did most evenings.

On the first evening Adriana was wearing a very classy white dress which was followed by another elegant outfit the next night as we all went to dinner. Adriana remembers:

I was pretty sure that Wes would propose soon, so I wanted to be ready for the surprise! But by the third day when nothing had happened, I decided just to relax and see what the Englishman was planning. Even so, I had another nice dress ready!

The Englishman was indeed busy planning. On the morning of the third day, I got up early with Raul and Jose as my co-conspirators to pick the time and the exact place of the proposed engagement.

The time I had in mind was sunset and the location was on the top of one of Cartagena's famous sea-facing walls. These high and thick battlements had taken two centuries to complete and had been strong enough to repulse Sir Francis Drake and other British invaders.

Now, I hoped they would be a place of romantic conquest for this Brit.

I took the precaution of finding a spot where a dropped ring could not fall down any ancient cracks never to be seen again. Next, having inquired at hotels and a music school, we finally found a saxophone player who agreed to accompany me at the crucial moment. And then we waited for the hours to tick by. I couldn't believe how young I was feeling nor how much simple fun this all was.

My plan was for "the guys" to go early into town while mother and daughter had some time together in the afternoon. Then we would all meet up for a meal at a nice restaurant later.

Adriana remembers:

I was happy to go along with these suggestions. I didn't suspect what was going on as everyone was so casual about everything.

Lina's job was to get her Mum to the wall just in time for those few minutes when the day's light gave way to a spectacular sunset. This she managed with perfect timing.

I positioned myself out of sight in a nearby café where I could watch the two of them arrive and walk up the ramparts. The boys went out to meet them and started taking some family pictures at the pre-arranged spot.

At this moment, I saw Adriana suddenly look around to see where the sound of a saxophone, playing one of her favourite Hispanic love songs, was coming from. Then, she broke into a very big smile as she quickly spotted that the saxophonist was walking towards her, accompanied by an Englishman dressed in a cream-coloured linen suit, smart shirt and tie.

Adriana recalls:

Instantly, I knew this was the moment of the engagement. I was so happy to see Wes. He looked really elegant and here he was coming for me. This was my dream becoming reality. The music and the whole scene were so romantic. Seriously, there were stars in my eyes, but no tears. I couldn't help laughing.

She laughed even more as I dropped to one knee, offered up the ring and came out with a question that I had been carefully practising in Spanish: *"Adriana, te casarías conmigo, por favor?"* (Will you marry me, please?)

Her answer was an immediate "Si!" I quickly got back to my feet to kiss my future bride.

Adriana remembers:

Actually, with the music I couldn't hear anything of what Wes was saying even though he had been practising his Spanish. But it was totally clear from his body language and the ring what he was asking. So, of course, I agreed to his official proposal.

Passers-by gathered round and offered their congratulations. We stayed on those walls for quite a time with Adriana and I holding each other close while trying to take in the perfection of the moment. This dream was real and getting better by the second.

After countless hugs and pictures, it was time for me to reveal the next stage of my engagement plan. I led Adriana carefully down to street level where horses and traditional carriages were waiting for us. I thought it was better for "the kids" to take the first carriage where we could watch them rather than the other way around.

By now the darkness had fallen, the lanterns were on, and we saw this UNESCO World Heritage Site up close and personal as our horses clip-clopped through the streets. This really was like being actors in a movie but there was nothing phoney about it.

I wished my family could have been here to enjoy this moment with us, especially my own "kids" who had been through so many different experiences with me.

I also found myself thinking about my long-departed Dad. I imagined him smiling at how his own journey from a little mining village in South Wales had now resulted in his son's new beginnings in far-off South America. I felt sure he and my Mum would have approved of the very special lady sitting close to me.

I pulled Adriana close to me with a considerable sense of gratitude and wonderment. And then we all alighted from our carriages, amidst the palm trees and enticing aromas, to celebrate our engagement under the stars in one of Cartagena's outstanding restaurants.

The party continued over the next few days, and we bonded as a new family and shared a lot of laughs lazing by the pool and the sea. But it was not all relaxation. Adriana and I quickly needed to focus. The wedding was now just one month away. We parted reluctantly, once more, with a very full diary of tasks and events ahead of us.

We continued with our twice daily FaceTime meetings as we coordinated all the typical wedding details of guests lists, seating plans, flowers, décor, and countless other matters.

In Bogotá, Adriana had some pre-wedding parties with her friends, one of which featured a touching video sent from my older grandkids. Isaac spoke for them all as he said: "We are looking forward to having a new grandma. We love you, Abuela."

In addition to all her bridal preparations, Adriana had a lot of transition to work through with clients in her business and in arranging handovers of her roles in the church.

I also had to make plans with the family and church as I would probably be away for the next three months or so. On my last Sunday in Windsor, I called onto the stage 12 faithful couples in the church and commissioned them as shepherds to help care for the flock.

Having done all that I could to put everything in order and get fitted for my bridegroom outfit, I once more flew back out to meet Adriana in the now very familiar Miami airport.

This time I did get a kiss when we met up. Actually, quite a few. Maybe I should have tilted my head evasively like Adriana had done on our first meeting, but I preferred to let bygones be bygones and make the most of the moment.

Pastors William and Liliana Raad were again a great support and shared in our mounting excitement as we worked our way through our many checklists and meetings. One particularly memorable appointment was at the Miami Beach Branch Court at Old City Hall. Here, within a few minutes, we received our licence to get married, after a remarkably simple process of producing our passports, basic details of our previous marriages, and handing over around 100 dollars.

We nearly bounced out of that place. We were so happy that we made even the previously-serious lady court clerk smile. And she was not alone. For, family and friends were arriving early to share in the joy and to make the most of this special time in Florida.

They came from Australia, the USA, South Africa, Burkina Faso, and of course from Colombia and the UK. We received many hugs, kind words, presents, and prayers. We had some very happy pre-wedding receptions together as we all waited, in mounting expectation, for the big day that Adriana had dreamed of for so long.

CHAPTER 10
O HAPPY DAY

I woke early on June 8, 2016, and looked out at a calm ocean by Miami Beach. The sun was shining, the pool attendants were putting out cushions on loungers and even the morning traffic on the opposite side of the hotel was moving freely.

It was a perfect day and an ideal setting for doing nothing. This was my plan for a few hours at least, knowing that everything was about to change in both my life and Adriana's life later that day.

After weeks of planning, I now had little to do but to savour the miracle of the moment. Adriana's schedule was naturally not so casual and included a morning full of appointments and preparations.

I sent some gifts to the wedding suite, including a bathrobe embossed with the name "Mrs. Richards".

Adriana remembers:

We were busy getting ready when three guys in smart suits suddenly arrived each holding a big box with a bow. I was so impressed that Wes had sent a special present for me and my two bridesmaids, Lina and Melody.

I felt like a film star sitting high up in the bridal apartment in my new bathrobe surrounded by make-up artists, manicurists, pedicurists, and hairstylists.

Since it was not necessary to allocate so much time to styling my own limited amount of hair (more a case of a quick polish), I headed downstairs for a celebratory breakfast with my adult children, Wesley, James, and Mel, who had taken temporary leave from her bridesmaid responsibilities. We had been through so many different experiences together, and I did not want to enter this new phase of my life, and theirs, without thanking them for being such an amazing support to me and to one another.

We reflected on how far we had all come and how God had taken us from being a depleted family to now having a very big family that was about to further extend in ways that we had never imagined.

After breakfast, I walked with my sons by the beach. I was touched by their words and felt the warmth of their love. "Matchmaker Mel" disappeared to coach Adriana in English for the personal vows that she wanted to make to me. Then it was my turn to spend some time alone in my room to write my own vows.

I was feeling so relaxed about everything that Wesley, James, Terry, and other friends popped in to inform me that I had better get a move on as Adriana was almost ready, ahead of time, to go for some photographs. With the British reputation for punctuality at risk, they banded together, to get me "suited and booted." Before I knew it, we were off for the "big moment" which had been arranged to take place in the classically designed Grand Promenade Room.

I was determined to take in every moment as I waited alongside my sons for my bride's arrival.

Everyone stood as my grandchildren, all immaculately dressed by their parents in matching outfits, proceeded down the aisle. Leading the way, confidently scattering petals on the white carpet, was my pretty eldest granddaughter Eliana, eldest daughter of James and Esther.

She was followed by the eldest grandsons, the cool looking "twin cousins," Samuel and Joseph, who were born within 75 hours of each other. We exchanged smiles as they did their best to support their grandad in this unexpected adventure.

Next in age were Isaac and Joel, who held their hands "prince-like," behind their backs and who gave me some quick grins as they passed me.

Wesley and Wilana's second son, Joshua, protectively accompanied his youngest brother, David, followed by the third brother, Daniel, walking next to his cousin, Caleb, both of them looking uncharacteristically angelic.

Wilana and Esther appeared next, each holding a twin in one arm with a hand extended reassuringly to Grace and Marianna.

So many blessings were represented in this family wedding procession. More came in the forms of the two beautiful bridesmaids in matching pink dresses, my daughter, Mel, and my new stepdaughter, Lina, each sharing a similar bouquet and common bond in bringing their dad and mum together.

My heart was overflowing with all these examples of God's goodness and mercy, but it was nearly overwhelmed when Adriana appeared. She glided into view on the arm of her brother, Carlos, to the sound of Bach's "Air on the G String."

Truly, I was transfixed when I saw Adriana. I was overwhelmed with emotion beyond what words or tears could convey. I stood there trying to comprehend the wonder of the "gift from God" who was walking straight towards me.

Adriana looked totally radiant and utterly stunning. I had never seen her so beautiful and so happy as she came and stood by my side. Adriana recalls:

It was the most exciting moment of my life to walk down the aisle with the support of my lovely brother. I was a little nervous when I saw all the families and friends and the pastors waiting for me. But, when I saw Wes standing so elegantly in his blue three-piece suit and yellow cravat, I was so happy, and I relaxed. He was my dream husband, and I was now going to marry him in my dream wedding dress.

As Carlos greeted me and joined Adriana's hand with mine, it was a moment of supreme restoration in our lives.

James stepped forward to open the ceremony and Wesley prayed a moving prayer. And then, as if on cue, the heavens opened, and a flash Florida storm hammered on the roofs and windows. We took this as a sign of God's favour and of abundant blessings to come.

The praise and worship songs we had chosen made it

easy to express what we were feeling and what we had experienced together to date. The first was, "This is Amazing Grace/Sublime Gracia" and contained these lines:

> *"Who brings our chaos back into order?*
> *Who makes the orphan a son and daughter?*
> *The King of Glory, the King above all Kings…*
> *This is amazing grace.*
> *This is unfailing love…"*[i]

The second song continued the theme of God's enduring love and faithfulness.

> *"You go before me, You're there beside me*
> *And if I wander your love will find Me.*
> *You go beside me, my Guardian."*[ii]

After reading from the "love chapter" of I Corinthians 13 by Wilana and Esther, our third song in Spanish was simply called "Una Nueva Historia" (A New Story).

My friend Dr Michael Peters, who was legally responsible for conducting the wedding ceremony, spoke first. Pete recalled how 14 years before, when we stood by the banks of the Missouri River in my time of deep sadness, he had told me, "Wes, you're going to make it."

He continued, "Today, you have made it. Today, a new book begins in your life. What chapters were unwritten now will be written with Adriana at your side."

Pete also spoke warmly of Adriana and recalled how 10 years earlier she had come to faith in Christ. Since then, she had shown "a covenant loyalty" in her faithfulness to God, her family and others. "Those who know you well, speak well of you. Your brother said just yesterday, 'I am so proud of my sister. She is a wonderful sister; a great mother and she will be a great wife.' Your children, Lina, Carlos, and Jose, support you because they have seen your faithfulness."

After those very personal and affirming words, Pete then did what I have done for so many couples over the years and asked the bridegroom to "repeat after him" the official marriage vows.

So, facing Adriana and holding her hand I said:

> *"I, Wes, take you, Adriana,*
> *To be my lawfully wedded wife*
> *To have and to hold*
> *From this day forward*
> *For better, for worse*
> *For richer, for poorer*
> *In sickness and in health*
> *To love and to cherish*
> *As long as we both shall live*
> *As God is my witness, I give you my promise."*

I was glad to have expressed each of these promises without faltering and I could see that this deeply impacted Adriana.

Then it was her turn to repeat these vows to me. I, too, now on the receiving end, felt the power of these simple declarations of lifelong, exclusive, and unconditional commitment.

Pastor César spoke next. He said: "I am so happy for this step that you are both taking today. A marriage is a miracle, but in this case I could say it is a mega-miracle. We could even make a movie out of this story.

"How could it be that two people who lived in such different places, in different cultures speaking different languages come together to get married in a nation that is neither one of your nations? But in God's timing, you have come together.

"It really is God's intervention. I know that there is a new future that is rising within you."

Pastor César shared how Jesus taught of the importance of building your house on a rock-like foundation that would withstand any storm. "When you are founded on a rock nothing will affect you. Your house will remain firm. Real success in marriage is when Jesus is the centre of your home. I know that you will have a very happy home. God will protect your minds, your words, and your attitudes."

After Pastor César's wise words, it was time to exchange our personal vows. I went first opening with what I trusted would be an impressive burst of Spanish:

"Mi amor, eres mi mas hermosa y preciosa Adriana (My love, you are my beautiful and precious Adriana). Hoy es el dia de jubileo y nuevo comienzo por nosotros (Today is a day of jubilee and a new beginning for us)."

In English, I told Adriana that I stood before her "amazed by the goodness and faithfulness of God. The

Lord has watched over us at every stage, and He will help us with every detail, every day." I continued:

"My darling, you are such a faithful, beautiful and loving person. You are a woman of noble character with great spiritual strength and sensitivity. I greatly respect and admire the way you have served your family and many other people. You are a true and wise woman of God with a vibrant personality and a great sense of humour.

"We have laughed so much together but we have also wiped tears from each other's eyes. We are perfect for one another, and I know that we will grow daily in our understanding and appreciation of one another."

I promised Adriana that, "With the help of the Holy Spirit I will be the best husband to you. I will listen to you since I know you are usually right… Not always but mostly.

"I will be gentle, kind, and attentive. I will pray often with you and always for you. I will be generous in every way. I will make you the best Colombian coffee in the morning.

"I will be faithful to you in my thoughts, speech and actions. And, of course, I will be very romantic towards you.

"Adriana, I promise to always hold you close and treasure you. Be very secure in my great love for you. I love you now and will love you always. (Te amo ahora y te amaré por siempre)."

Adriana surprised me by speaking with no notes. She began by thanking God, "because we all can feel His presence and His love. I'm so grateful to God for writing our story. I want to give thanks to God because I know He prepared all this."

Adriana then addressed her thanks to me.

"I'm so grateful to you for loving God, for being so committed to God, for keeping yourself all these years. You are such a special man. You are so sincere. You are a very faithful man. You're a very intelligent man and I know that you will be the best husband.

"I am so grateful to you because you are very romantic and you're so generous. You really knew how to get me to fall in love with you.

"You are a man that loves family just as much as I love family. We have very similar tastes in so many things. I know that we will be a great complement to one another. I'm so grateful for you making this dream come to pass because you worked hard on it and now is your time for reward.

"Today, I want to promise you that I will be a very special wife to you, and I will always demonstrate my love for you. I will always be generous in every one of my actions.

"I will be generous with my words, with my prayers for you, for our families, and for all the people around us. I want to promise you that I will be with you at all times. I will always be on your side. I will be with you. I will always help you in whatever you need."

Adriana then finished her vows with some words that I was not expecting. They were taken from the book of Ruth. Adriana looked directly at me as she said slowly in well-rehearsed English: "Where you go I will go, where you stay I will stay. Your people will be my people, and your God will be my God."[1]

In a ceremony of many powerful moments, this was, for me, the most unforgettable of them all. For it was now clear to each other and to everyone watching that we both were doing far more than joining together in a "contract" of marriage. We were declaring our decision to make an irrevocable *covenant* of lifelong union serving God together. All this was sealed as we exchanged rings, received communion, and had additional prayers and blessings spoken over us.

It was then time for the new "Mr. and Mrs. Richards" to celebrate with all the gathered family and friends. As we turned around to exit the service, the song Adriana had chosen quickly created a festive Latin atmosphere. It was written by a couple who had also married within a few months of meeting and was called *"Ella es mi fiesta" (She is my party).* We danced back up the aisle and, from that moment on, the party spirit seemed to fill the air.

We had a great time striking poses, in various family combinations, for the multiple wedding photographs. One of the most memorable was of Adriana and I holding the twins while the other eleven grandchildren gathered around us. Somehow, they all managed to look at the camera at the same time.

Eventually, with the last of the bride and groom pictures taken, we made our way up to the wedding reception in the spectacular Starlight Room at the top of the hotel. Its floor-to-ceiling windows offered spectacular

---

[1]. Ruth 1:16

panoramic views over the Miami skyline and the Atlantic Ocean. As darkness fell, the 16-foot-high ceilings lit up with a myriad of lights giving the impression of being out under the stars.

Everyone was relaxed and joyful. All the children seemed very happy with their own party bag and "big table" which was near to our head table for two. Family and friends stopped by to greet us including my two-and-a-half-year-old granddaughter, Grace, whose life had hung in the balance just a few years earlier. She spontaneously jumped on my lap for a big hug.

The speeches from our children and various pastors were full of fond memories and good wishes. Then Yajaira Zutta, Adriana's long-time friend and hairdresser who had led her so faithfully through different stages of her spiritual development, stepped up to sing. She sang a famous Latin Christian song by Marcela Gándara called "Un Largo Viaje," or "A Long Trip." She was clearly moved as she sang. My bride was also quietly wiping away her tears. Only when I later read the translation did I understand why. Some of the lines were particularly expressive of Adriana's journey to find love.

After this emotional moment, the mood shifted with a change in music. A wave of approval swept through the guests as Adriana and I stepped up for our first dance. Mercifully, Adriana quickly and discreetly gave me a few helpful tips since we did not have time to practise. Fortunately for me, we danced to a slower tune instead of fast Salsa music from Adriana's home city of Cali. The video later revealed that we moved together smoothly - an undoubted relief for me as few Brits can compete with the natural rhythm of a Colombian.

Next, the grandkids - who had already displayed remarkable stamina - and the adults from all the different nations, joined us on the dance floor to conclude an unforgettable international family fiesta. Finally, everyone joined hands, forming a "tunnel of love" for us to walk through before we completed a long round of goodbyes. True to Colombian tradition, we came back for even more hugs before finally making our exit.

We checked out of the wedding hotel, where most of our guests were based, and headed to our "secret destination" as I used to call it when I was a young wedding reporter. We settled into our nearby hotel. And there we stayed, happily undisturbed for a few days.

CHAPTER 11
A VERY DIFFERENT KIND OF HONEYMOON

Adjusting to married life after so many years of being single was a joyful but sometimes startling experience. One honeymoon morning, as I slowly emerged from a deep sleep, I was aware of someone snuggled close to me. I groggily opened my eyes to see that it was a stunning and not altogether fully dressed lady.

I must have been very disorientated, for I momentarily panicked. *Oh God,* I thought, *what have I done? Who is this woman? Oh no, this is the end of my ministry!*

Hazily, I began to remember my newly married status. I breathed a deep sigh of relief as I gazed upon my very recent and special gift from God. And then, reassured that all was well with my soul, I began to shake with so much laughter that I woke up my sleeping beauty.

One of the biggest adjustments to married life was not just learning to adapt to one another, but also figuring out how to simultaneously integrate our families; our six children, children-in-law and all their children.

The first stage of our honeymoon was carefully balanced between us having time alone and making the most of the rare opportunity for our families to all be together in Florida with all its fun and theme parks. Both Adriana and I had fond memories of taking our children to these parks when they were younger, but neither of us could quite believe we were back here with them as adults and, in my case, also with their children.

Adriana had told me she had always prayed for a large family, but she never expected having a family this big which had arrived all in one package and in one moment. Happily, the grandkids quickly adopted their new "Abuela." They competed to go on rides with her and to try out the few words of Spanish they had learned in school. They also had great fun reuniting with Aunty Lina and playing with their two new "uncles," Adriana's sons, Carlos and Jose.

They were eager to make up for lost time with Grandad, sharing hugs and catching up after I had so suddenly vanished out of their lives during the whirlwind weeks of long-distance romance.

On one memorable day we gathered for a UK/Colombian/South African family picture in the Main Street of Disney's Magic Kingdom. I marvelled at how our families were being rebuilt and blessed in ways that we could never have imagined.

Even as we were celebrating together, there were further romantic developments. Lina was about to be rewarded for her selfless and brave prayer: *"Lord please let my Mum get married before me. I don't want her to be at home alone."* Raul, no doubt relieved that he did not have to wait long for his girlfriend's prayer to be answered, chatted with us about temporarily excusing himself from the family festivities.

Just as Lina had done a great job helping with her Mum's surprise engagement, Adriana now smoothed the way for Raul to take her beloved daughter to a beautiful Florida beach where he made his own romantic proposal.

Having pre-set his camera so that we could all later witness the moment, they drove back to show us the photos and ring and share their plans for another family wedding early the following year.

These various carefree times, together with meals out, barbecues, and South African style braais, helped to quickly bond our large new family. There were babies who needed constant attention, toddlers prone to confidently wandering off to explore unfamiliar territory, younger kids excited and ready for any fresh adventures, and the adult "big kids" who were making rapid adjustments as parents and grandparents.

Once more it felt like we were in a movie. This time we seemed to be featuring in our very own family comedy like *Cheaper by the Dozen* or *Yours, Mine and Ours,* where two widowed parents marry and try to figure out a new life with their combined groups of children. At the time of our marriage, we had 14 grandchildren between us, my 13 and Adriana's granddaughter, Maria Camilla, who by a few months became the oldest grandchild.

Samuel, who had previously held that title and Joseph, just 75 hours younger than his cousin, took their demotion well.

With this wonderful, diverse, noisy, happy and loving family around us, I was able to celebrate my 66th birthday as a very blessed and contented man. I felt thankful beyond words for each one of them. They, and especially Adriana, were making me feel so many years younger than my actual age. I was being renewed for a brand new season of life and also for the next stage of our honeymoon after we had all said our family goodbyes for the summer.

Jose had discovered an excellent online deal for us - a two-week Caribbean cruise out of Miami. The ship's name summed up what we were experiencing. It was called *Divina* or "divine." It was a massive Italian ship which had been launched by Hollywood legend Sophia Loren.

With 18 decks and over 4,000 passengers on board, the *MSC Divina* somehow managed to combine multiple popular attractions with an impressive aura of European style and culture.

There was a real stone piazza, a magnificent theatre, an exhibition of La Dolce Vita photographs, and elegant Swarovski crystal staircases.

The staircases found instant favour with Adriana. She took great delight in walking up and down them as often as possible, especially in the evenings when she wore her best dresses and, of course, looked exquisite. It took my best attempts at translation to explain to Adriana that such staircases were not a usual feature in British homes.

Adriana told me more of her own Italian roots. She explained how she had always wanted to visit the homeland of her paternal grandfather who came from Tuscany, but she had not wanted to do so until she could visit with a romantic husband. She shared how much she enjoyed Italian food, especially mozzarella and tomato, prosciutto, pasta with pesto and especially seafood risotto. With many different types of Italian restaurants on board, some in surprisingly very cosy spaces on this big ship, I could see that we were well set for some very intimate meals together.

I was impressed at how all these various ingredients of the Italian experience were making my wife so relaxed. With the least excuse, even in public, she would frequently blow kisses at me. Naturally, I played along. I did my best to be the suave and attentive continental suitor complete with shrugged shoulders and inviting eyes. Mostly my impressions had Adriana rolling her eyes in amused disbelief. But she got the basic message and swayed along as Italian opera music played in the background.

However, Adriana totally failed to comprehend why I started singing, "there's one cornetto, it's Walls Ice Cream" to the tune of the Neapolitan opera song *0 Sole Mio.* (Check out the Walls cornetto British tv commercial on YouTube to envisage the impression I was trying to make).

Undoubtedly, our onboard romantic experience was helped by us having our own spacious stateroom where we could retreat into our own very comfortable private world. Our original cabin could certainly be described as intimate since there was just enough space for us to manoeuvre around our suitcases. After our first night, when there had been excessive noise above us, I called the ship's office to see if we could switch rooms.

The manager who spoke to me was a helpful young lady with an unmistakable South African accent. She listened with great interest as I told her of our family's links to South Africa and the stories of the three weddings. Finally, we got on to the reason for my call. Within an hour, she had us upgraded at no extra cost. We were moved to a large, stylishly carpeted suite with its own dressing table, lounge, and a sizable ocean-facing balcony. This was the perfect place to unwind after the busy months of long-distance travel and non-stop events, exciting as all this was. Favour for sure.

We felt totally relaxed as our "love boat" carried us from one idyllic Caribbean location to the next. Days and nights floated by timelessly as we visited Puerto Rico, St. Thomas, the U.S. Virgin Islands, St. Maarten, the Bahamas, Jamaica, the Cayman Islands, and Mexico. This was the longest time we had yet been together on our own. It was both a pleasure and a necessity to have this opportunity to develop our friendship and love.

We soon adjusted to the nightly routine of getting dressed up and walking hand-in-hand to the late sitting for dinner. People would greet us as if we were a well-established couple. Without Lina around to help us with the translation, we had to figure out many ways to overcome the big language barrier between us.

We soon drew quizzical stares from fellow diners as we sat at our table for two passing a phone back and forth between us. It would not have been immediately obvious that we were looking at a translation app trying to understand what we were saying to each other. Sometimes we would even act out what we were trying to communicate as if we were addicted to playing charades.

The distinguished head manager noticed this unusual activity and came over to discreetly check what was going on. Fortunately, he spoke English and Spanish, and we were able to quickly explain our love story. His previously somewhat formal mood instantly changed. As an Italian, he was immediately enthusiastic and demonstrative. He politely kissed Adriana's hand and congratulated me, with what I thought was a look of faint disbelief, that I had won the heart of such a beautiful lady.

He became like a big brother and would always find a great table for us. In mock-seriousness he would express concern if we were even so much as a minute late for a meal. He would inquire, with raised eyebrows, if there was any particular activity that had detained us. Every day he seemed happy to see us growing closer as a couple despite our near total non-comprehension of each other's native language. This of course could and did lead to some classic misunderstandings.

In one seemingly serene moment, Adriana leaned over to me and suddenly announced, "I am angry, really angry."

I was at a total loss to understand what I had done to cause her displeasure. "Why are you angry with me, Mi Amor?" I asked, trying to reassure her of my love with some limited Spanish.

"No, no" Mi Amor replied, "A-n-g-u-r-y, no food!"

"Oh, hungry," I said both enlightened and relieved.

On another occasion, Adriana had to choose to continue believing that I truly wanted to help her in every way, despite a painful misunderstanding. She had asked me to help her with a hot dish. I understood that Adriana wanted me to choose one for her. I was therefore quickly studying the menu as a piping hot meal arrived, totally failing to notice that Adriana was struggling in some discomfort to hold it.

A little knowledge, it soon became clear, was indeed dangerous. For example, I imagined that I understood what she was saying when she used the Spanish word, "compromiso." To me it obviously meant compromise.

Adriana said she wanted our marriage to have a lot of "compromiso" to God and each other.

"No, I countered; we should never compromise and settle for less than the best."

Adriana looked confused. Finally, we arrived at an understanding of our misunderstanding - "compromiso" did not mean "compromise" as I had assumed, but rather "commitment". We reaffirmed that we were definitely *committed* to each other and would never compromise on our principles.

The potential to cause unwitting hurt led to us making an early pact that we would always believe the best about each other even if, in the moment, we couldn't make sense of each other.

We also were learning fast that you can do a lot to build a relationship by discovering the simple power of a look, a smile, a laugh, a gesture, and of course a touch.

For a man of words since my days as a journalist, I began to think that verbal expression was perhaps overrated. Maybe we had accidently hit on the perfect way for a husband and wife to communicate.

The wife is free to say whatever she wants to say without fear of interruption while her husband looks at her with complete contentment and nods appreciatively at regular intervals. The husband, in turn, can sound forth on any subject without fear of misunderstanding or argument while the wife gazes adoringly at her wise and omniscient husband.

In our case, any real or imagined offence wasn't worth discussing anyway since it took so much time and effort to translate. How long such a peace accord could last, we didn't know but for the moment it was obviously working very well.

One older couple we met on the cruise remarked on how happy we looked together. The husband, however, drew me aside for a quiet word. He was from South Wales, like my father. He asked in an accent so familiar to me, "Is your wife ok? She seems lovely and smiles a lot, but she doesn't say anything."

"Well, that's because she doesn't really have any idea of what we are talking about," I answered. "She only speaks Spanish and I only speak English."

"Well, however do you understand each other?" he said, looking concerned.

"Look my friend," I replied, "how long have you and your wife been married?"

"Over 30 years…"

"And do you understand your wife?"

He just smiled and nodded his head in agreement.

Back in the UK, we discovered others were expressing their concern about whether we would be "lost at sea" with our honeymoon communication. Pastor César was having great fun telling our story at a conference that I had been due to host before we planned our wedding. "Now they don't have Lina with them and there is no Wi-Fi on a cruise ship far out to sea, whatever will they do? However, will they be able to communicate?" he asked, to widespread laughter, the loudest of which I recognised as coming from members of my own family. As it happened, we were able to buy a Wi-Fi package and were amused to observe the jokes being made at our expense as we sat sipping cool drinks on our sun loungers.

Of course, we were happy enough not to be at the conference at that moment, but even in the midst of all our honeymoon celebrations, we did not miss out on some powerful spiritual experiences together.

One language we clearly did share was the language of prayer. One of the fixed points of each of our lives for many years was daily morning and evening prayer. So, with all the changes that we were juggling, we both found it reassuring to be kneeling together by our bed and taking turns to pray, albeit in different languages. It was like we were two young kids from the same family both confidently speaking and listening to our Father who could easily understand both of us even if we couldn't understand each other.

On the longest stretch of our cruise far out to sea, we

shared a memorable experience of the presence of the Holy Spirit. Adriana recalls:

For over two days and nights we had seen only water, water, water. As I sat out on the balcony for several hours, I began to realise, as never before, just how big the ocean was. I never imagined its dimensions. I couldn't see any beginning or end. It was so deep and wide and seemed to reach to the sky. God showed me that this was what His love was like for the world and for me. I felt overwhelmed and couldn't stop crying.

When Adriana managed to explain to me why she had been crying I told her of a famous hymn, "Here is love, Vast as the Ocean," the 'love song' of the great 1904 spiritual revival in Wales. I translated the words and then softly sang them to her.

> *Here is love, vast as the ocean*
> *Loving kindness as the flood*
> *When the Prince of Life, our Ransom*
> *Shed for us His precious blood*[i]

Adriana's tears continued to flow as she, like countless generations before her, was touched by the powerful lines of one of my favourite hymns.

> *On the mount of crucifixion*
> *Fountains opened deep and wide*
> *Through the floodgates of God's mercy*
> *Flowed a vast and gracious tide*
> *Grace and love, like mighty rivers*
> *Poured incessant from above*
> *And Heaven's peace and perfect justice*

Kissed a guilty world in love.[ii]

These tender moments together mellowed our hearts and undoubtedly made us more sensitive to one another. We promised each other to always do all we could to keep God's love flowing between us and to willingly embrace every adaptation that we would need to make… big or small.

CHAPTER 12
LONG HOT SUMMER OF LOVE

For me one of the most unexpected changes on the honeymoon was to drink a cup of coffee for the first time. I had just never liked it. But my Colombian bride felt that drinking coffee together was an essential ingredient for a happy marriage.

So, on one sun kissed day in a quaint café in Old San Juan, Puerto Rico, I broke with the habit of a lifetime and told her to go ahead and order a special brand from her homeland. I tasted it slowly. And it was good, just as my wife had promised.

We both enjoyed this new experience of relaxing and drinking a lot of coffee together over the following weeks. Mostly we did so in very warm locations. Thanks to a prolonged leave of absence, we were able to spend our very own "summer of love" in tropical climates.

One of the first hot spots we visited after the cruise was Cali, home of Adriana's very large extended family, most of whom had not been able to come to Miami. As a result, it was agreed that we would have a second wedding celebration for all to enjoy.

This was my first visit to Cali, and I quickly became a fan of the city. At first, I was relieved not to have been kidnapped on arrival after having heard many dire stories about the place. I soon discovered, however, that we were able to safely stroll around many areas such as the popular and quaintly named "Chipichape" shopping mall.

As soon as we stepped out of the air-conditioned airport, it was easy to feel relaxed. The heat seemed to wrap itself around you straight away, and the people were laid back and friendly. The warmth of welcome from the family for their new foreign relative was instant. Adriana's brother, Carlos Alberto, my new *hermano*, greeted me as if I was a long established and much-loved family member.

It was emotional to meet Adriana's father, Carlos Batidas, who had not been able to come to the wedding in Miami. At first sight of his newly married daughter, he wept over her and hugged her tightly. Then he held out his arms to embrace me and said in the few words of English that he had learnt, "You are now my English son. Now I will like Manchester United, and you will like Deportivo Cali." This famous football team was passionately supported by all the family, including my wife, and it was expected, if not commanded, that I would now join their numbers and not show any interest in their key rival, America de Cali.

I felt like a prize exhibit as I was introduced to family members who seemed to grow in number by the day.

However, without knowing much Spanish or the humour of the locals, I felt a little disadvantaged.

Over one lunch, Monica, an English-speaking businesswoman and the wife of my new brother-in-law, Carlos, smiled as she gently told me, "We are so pleased to meet you. We really love Adriana and we have always wanted the best husband for her." Then she leaned forward, pointed her fingers first to her eyes and then to me, and added slowly, "… So just remember, we will be watching you!" Maybe it was some negative images of Colombia that were quickly surfacing from my subconscious, but I found the words of the sweet Monica slightly menacing. *Was she joking?*

I was also not totally reassured at the way she and the whole family were so enthusiastic for me to sample their speciality called "Sancocho Valluno" (pronounced va-joo-noh). That means "Soup from the Valley." This soup consisted of lots of plantain, different potatoes, and various cuts of beef. It was tasty enough but eating hot soup in such a hot climate took some getting used to.

For different reasons, I was sweating at new levels. I asked, "Seriously, is it usual for you to eat like this in summer?"

"Yes," they said, "it is summer every day of the year in Cali. Just try it."

I asked suspiciously why they were all so insistent that I should be the first to taste the soup while they all waited expectantly for my reaction. They laughed, Adriana especially, as they sensed my apprehension. Anyway, I lived to tell the story, albeit with somewhat burnt lips.

I was also quickly warming up to the many members of my new Colombian family. Aunty Nubia, sister of Adriana's mum, who had died at such a young age, was particularly welcoming. She, together with Aunty Fabia and Aunty Ruth, who lives in Europe, had been like surrogate mums to my bride. Aunty Nubia reminded me of my late and kindly grandmother, Lucy, from Nottinghamshire who had affectionately called everyone "duck."

The wedding celebration was hosted at the home of Marilyn, a long-time friend of Adriana. Her beautiful home was situated in the hills and had spectacular views of the city. She and her family treated us all royally. Her catering was of the highest quality as were the spectacular flower arrangements. The centrepiece of the table was the largest paella I had ever seen and included numerous huge lobsters and prawns.

Adriana wore her wedding dress a second time and arrived with her characteristic perfect hairstyling and make up. The celebration began with her dad, his back straight, proudly walking arm-in-arm with Adriana. He came close to me and through the interpreter he said, "Wes, I give you my treasure. She is very special to me. Please look after her all your life."

I promised that I would honour his request and try to be, "the best husband."

Adriana recalled:

I was overjoyed to be back home in Cali among my family and friends with the husband that I had prayed for over so many years. It was such a sign to me of how God had totally turned my life around. He brought me back to the place where I had known a lot of sadness, loneliness and difficulties. Now I was beginning a new life of great restoration and healing in my heart. And I could see that so many miracles were also happening in the lives of my family.

For me, all this seemed like a personalised modern-day version of Psalm 126:1-3: "When the Lord restored the fortunes of Zion, we were like those who dreamed. Our mouths were filled with laughter, our tongues with songs of joy."

Some of the laughter of our visit was often at my expense, not least when we made an early trip to a famous spot overlooking Cali and featuring a statue of its founder, Sebastián de Belalcázar. While we were there, a national TV company was making a trailer for a new soap opera. This featured a group of Mexican-dressed musicians, or Mariachis Mexicanos. Clearly, as the only "gringo" around, I stood out amongst a big group of onlookers. Before I knew it, the director spotted me, grabbed my arm, and placed a huge sombrero on my head. Then he handed me a microphone to say a few words. My protests that I did "no hablo español" were swept aside. I looked to Adriana for help only to find that she had quickly vanished into the crowd.

Adriana recounts:

I was nervous about being pulled in, so I disappeared temporarily forgetting that I was now married and needed to support Wes. I felt a bit guilty, but I was sure that somehow, he would cope.

Having spotted that my darling, nervous bride was not so far away after all, I decided to go for it and rapidly spoke a few imperfect phrases of Spanish with as much "entusiasmo" as I could manage, which seemed to greatly amuse everyone.

We survived this early divergence as a couple, and we laughed about being caught up in this ridiculous spectacle. But it was not long before we had to negotiate yet another misunderstanding.

Thanks to Adriana accumulating many points on a hotel scheme which she had never used, we were able to spend several weeks at various stunning locations, among them the outstanding Coral Island of San Andres, with its famous "seven shades of blue" in its waters.

One tranquil morning while Adriana lounged on a palm tree-fringed beach, I decided to dip my feet into the Caribbean Sea. I was not planning to swim as I had my glasses on. Unfortunately, I hadn't noticed a rock and, when I did, I instinctively dived over it. Surfacing, I realised that I had lost my glasses, and, in my blurred state, I frantically swished around to find them. Having no success, I shouted out for help. "Adriana. Come. Now." But Adriana didn't come. So, in some desperation I shouted two or three times more, in between dipping up and down and continuing my search.

Adriana remembers:

I couldn't believe that Wes was being so rude shouting at me from the sea. I thought, 'Wow, this is no way to treat your wife.' So, I decided not to go to him. But when he shouted more, I went to see him out of embarrassment. When he explained what had happened and that he needed my help, I felt so sorry for him.

Despite both of us searching some more and engaging the skills of a local diver, my designer glasses floated away never to be seen again. From that moment, like the half-healed blind man in the Bible, I only saw "men as trees walking."[1]

Adriana therefore took over the driving of the golf buggy around the island and pointed out various outstanding spots. "Look, isn't that beautiful?" she would say.

"I don't know. I can't see," I replied, trying not to be irritable with my new and lovely wife.

Adriana not only saw the wonders of this island paradise but also the funny side of her Englishman's lost glasses. Her infectious, and not totally sympathetic, laughter at my predicament soon lightened my mood. We managed to find some antiquated owl-like glasses at a local optician, which did nothing for my image, but which helped to bring my wife and my life back into focus. Adriana recalls:

In more relaxed surroundings, I apologised to Wes for jumping to the wrong conclusion. We agreed that we needed to learn from this incident. We saw that we really needed to always stay disciplined so that we would believe the best of each other in whatever circumstances we found ourselves in.

After San Andres, with new glasses on order, we couldn't wait to get back to Cartagena, the scene of our engagement, for our first visit as a married couple. With all the busyness and planning of the wedding behind us, we could now relax in the late afternoons and evenings,

---

1. Mark 8:24

strolling down the now familiar historic streets, and enjoying the balmy sea breezes as we ate outdoors at various restaurants.

If the nights were heavenly, the days in contrast were much more down-to-earth. For in these lazy, hazy days we had to face the reality of a looming deadline of an English exam that Adriana needed to pass to receive a visa to return with me to the UK. We had less than 10 days to get her ready for this.

Adriana had a lot of faith that she would pass. "No problem. I believe," she said confidently in the very limited English that she knew. Knowing how much she did not know, I nevertheless, did not want to say anything negative. But I understood very clearly that we urgently needed to combine faith with some considerable work.

Late one night, while Adriana was sleeping soundly, trusting in God, I applied myself to researching the exams that she would have to take. I did a google search to study the different sections in each exam. Then, having compared several years of exams, I wrote out a list of questions that I thought Adriana would most likely be asked and scripted some answers that she could give.

Our training ground where we spent many long hours, was a beautifully designed old library, the *Biblioteca Bartolomé Calvo*, named after a 19th century president. Our favourite spot was a little area upstairs directly under a paddle fan. It was here, while trying to cope with the sweltering heat, that Adriana diligently applied herself to learning various answers by rote.

"Where do you live?"

- *I live near a park in a beautiful part of Bogotá.*

"What are your hobbies?"

- *I like to go shopping, visit nice restaurants and watch good movies. I also spend a lot of my time going to a very large church.*

"What is your favourite book?

- *My favourite book is Pride and Prejudice by Jane Austen.*

Understanding these questions and mastering the answers with clear pronunciation was far more difficult than either of us imagined and required a lot of mutual patience. Thankfully, we passed that test at least, stopping regularly to enjoy more coffee together.

Finally, when I was reasonably sure that Adriana had learnt her lines, I counselled her to be sure to listen to the questions carefully in order to avoid giving the wrong pre-programmed answer.

"For example," I said, "if they ask you what your favourite book is, please don't answer, 'I live in a beautiful part of Bogotá' or 'I like to go shopping.' Also, like a politician, try to answer a question with one of the answers you have already prepared."

When we arrived back in Bogotá for the test, we took it as a hopeful sign that it was being held in a hotel called

Windsor House. I waited prayerfully in the lobby for the return of my "student" who I wanted to take home with me to Windsor, England.

Adriana was beaming as she came out. "I am sure I passed. God helped me with options that I didn't know, and I used the phrases you taught me."

"Aha," I said with a smile of satisfaction. "Did you give the answer I taught you about your favourite book?"

Adriana waved her hand dismissively, and said with some superiority, "Yes, of course, I told them it was *Pride and Prejudice*, by Joel Osteen." At that moment I felt I needed to lie down.

Within a week, however, despite confusing a famous English author with a best-selling American preacher, Adriana was shrieking with joy as she opened the official letter confirming that she had indeed passed her exam. Even with the considerable amount of prayer and work that we had put in, I felt that this was right up there in the realm of "miraculous." Seriously, Adriana really didn't know much English at this point.

Throughout the summer, we travelled back and forth from different laid-back locations to Bogotá, a city which was often far from relaxing. From mid-August through mid-September, it became our base. This, in turn, gave us the opportunity to attend Lina's graduation as she finally received her degree in aeronautical engineering and to reflect on the significance of her study time in England.

Spending an extended time in the busy capital and becoming more accustomed to daily life there was very different from visiting for several days at a conference. I have travelled to many places, but this was one of the rare times that I felt some real cultural dislocation.

Since the wedding, I was now being treated like a local rather than a foreigner, both by many new friends that I was introduced to, as well as family members. They now accepted me as one of their own, and they seemed to imagine that this conferred on me an instant fluency in Spanish. Consequently, they would talk to me freely and rapidly in a language I barely understood. Like Adriana on our honeymoon cruise, I learnt to smile a lot to disguise my almost total incomprehension. Their pleasure at my apparent ability to grasp what they were saying of course only encouraged them to speak even more freely and rapidly.

Adriana would not only chat with people at great speed but also, despite the constant and dispiriting heavy traffic, would move with great efficiency from one appointment to another. It was impressive seeing how much she accomplished so quickly in her own familiar world. I, however, felt increasingly out of sorts.

On one occasion, I found myself meekly following Adriana and Lina into their local and large hairdressers which also served as a centre for manicures and pedicures. Before I knew it, my wife and stepdaughter vanished for their own appointments. Some unknown ladies in white coats then came to me and gestured for me to sit by a wash basin. Then, without my permission or any explanation, they took off my shoes and socks, placed my feet in a bowl of water and spread my hands out on side trays. I felt like an abandoned soul in an end-times *Left Behind* movie. After what felt like several hours, Adriana, who had seemingly been raptured to heaven, had an epiphany. "Oh yes, I have a husband that I arrived with. Where is he?" She returned to find me seated in some bewilderment with newly cut and trimmed nails surrounded by some smirking staff.

This experience, like several others in Colombia, emphasised to me just how many adjustments and emotions are involved in making the transition from being secure in your own language and world to feeling so vulnerable in another culture. For me this was only a temporary experience. For Adriana, it was about to become an ongoing challenge as she would permanently uproot from everything she knew.

I promised myself that I would not forget what it was like to feel like a stranger in a foreign land, and that I would do all that I could to help Adriana to feel at home in the new and very different world in the UK that she was soon about to enter.

CHAPTER 13
A YEAR OF JUBILEE

The last day before we left Bogotá for the UK, our future together was marked in an unexpected and powerful way. After so many years on my own as a pastor, we were very publicly launched into a new ministry together as a couple.

We were packing our cases when we received an invitation from Pastor César's office. He invited us to preach at the 7, 9, and 11 a.m. Sunday services of MCI. This meant that we would be addressing a combined total of around 25,000 people.

It had always been a privilege to speak in Adriana's home church at various large services and conference events. On many of those occasions, Adriana had been out there listening somewhere among the vast crowd. But now she was being asked to take a big step up onto that very large platform alongside me.

Adriana told me the biggest events that she had previously spoken at were attended by "only smaller gatherings of 1000 people." I was fascinated by her definition of "small" which is far bigger than most UK churches. Nevertheless, she handled this new challenge with ease as if she had been preparing for this for all along - which was indeed the case.

Each of the services followed a similar pattern. When I was introduced, I was warmly received. But, when the moment came to introduce my new wife, one of their own, the noise levels went to another level as they gave her a very enthusiastic Latino welcome.

They listened intently and applauded frequently as we each gave our accounts of how our Colombian/British love story had unfolded. The theme we had chosen was one which clearly resonated with the people. It was called, "Go for the Best and Never Give Up."

The Bible passage we used was taken from 2 Kings 13:14-20. This story tells how the great prophet Elisha instructed the King of Israel to take some arrows and to hit the ground with them. The arrows represented victory. The King did this three times and then stopped. This did not please Elisha.

Verse 19 says, "The man of God was angry with him and said, 'You should have struck the ground five or six times; then you would have defeated Aram and completely destroyed it. But now you will defeat it only three times.'"

Our message was focussed on never settling for second-best. Since God has the best plans for us, we must persist until we receive everything that He has for us.

I told how I had needed to decide not to give up after

the death of my first wife from cancer, when neither I nor our three children knew how we would get through this heart-breaking time. Adriana shared her sadness of having a broken marriage at the age of 24 and how difficult it had been for her to bring up three young children. Yet, for all our pain, each of us as single people had continued to believe that, with God's help, we could still have the best in life.

I said: "We never gave up hope, and we stand before you today, not just to tell you about our story, but to give you hope for your story, because God has no favourites. You too can know his amazing grace. Just don't give up."

Adriana then addressed everyone directly in Spanish. She said: "Nine years ago I came to this church for the very first time. I was like many of you are today, but I accepted God's call to me. This is where God began to transform my life. From this day on, this is the place where He will begin to transform your life, and your family's life. Just believe Him and do what I did. Just as God worked wonders in my life, I am sure that He's going to work wonders in your life."

We next invited people to come forward for prayer if they wanted to give their lives fully to the Lord and to receive his best blessings.

I shall never forget what happened in these moments, towards the end of each of the three services. People started to stream forward from all parts of the building; first in trickles, which quickly became like a flood in every aisle, until many hundreds of people stood before us for prayer. People from all walks of life responded… men and women, singles, couples, older, but mostly younger people. Many had tears pouring down their faces as they asked God to work miracles in their lives.

I, too, could not hold back my tears. I had seen this kind of response before in big events with the evangelist Billy Graham. But this was different. It was taking place in one local church that had started with just eight people in a hostile spiritual environment. I visualised this also happening in the UK and recognised, with great clarity in that moment, that Adriana and I had been brought together for much more than our personal romantic happiness.

The emotion of the weekend was heightened when, having previously said our farewells to Adriana's sons and her family in Cali, it was now time to say goodbye to Lina, who had always been very close to her Mum and who had played such a key role as our relationship developed.

Adriana recalls:

We cried over one another, but I was happy to know that Lina would soon be married, and that God had given a new beginning not just for me but all our family.

As we left for the journey home via Florida, we both felt peaceful and excited for the next chapter of our story. In Miami, we stayed overnight at the hotel where we had married seemingly an age before. We reminisced with great thankfulness on all the blessings that we had received. It seemed strange not to have the wedding party with us. They had all moved on and now, we too were ready for the next stage of our journey.

Even as we flew out of Miami, we were reminded of God's favour. The American booking agent, having briefly heard our story, gave us complimentary upgrades and wished us well. He smiled reassuringly as he handed us our tickets as he said, "I too married a wonderful Colombian lady years ago. It's been a great marriage."

Happily refreshed after resting in business class beds, we were fully awake and able to enjoy the moment of our arrival at Heathrow. We were met by a large welcome party consisting of family, friends and church members who greeted us noisily with banners, balloons, flowers, and hugs.

I was delighted to see Adriana being made to feel so at home. For me, reconnecting with everyone was truly special. However, amidst the rapid changes, we were reminded of the reality that we didn't have a home of our own to live in for the time being.

We couldn't move back into my house right away. My daughter, son-in-law, and their five children were still living there, as they had done for many years. Of course, we were not about to evict them. In time, they would find a lovely place of their own nearby and Adriana, an experienced interior designer, would beautifully and totally transform our house and garden. But for now, we would be like a young couple starting out in temporary accommodation.

My bride showed a remarkable adaptability to her new life as we settled into a quaint English village near Henley, famed as the home of the world's most famous rowing regatta. Thanks to the kindness of Richard and Louise Beasley, Terry and Margaret's son and daughter-in-law, and their son Isaac, we were able to stay in a cozy summer house with a small loft bedroom. While I wish I could have brought my princess back to a castle of her own, Adriana made our limited space feel like home, affectionately naming our first marital residence, "The Doll's House."

One benefit of our country retreat was that we managed to relax and enjoy walks along the nearby River Thames during some very pleasant early autumn weather. Adriana said:

For me it was a perfect introduction to a very English way of life. The traffic in Bogotá seemed far away and we couldn't even hear the planes from Heathrow. We loved this special time of peace and quiet in our little nest. We were so happy just to be together and to let everything work out.

Her public introduction to the church, and my reintroduction after being away for such a long time, came on our first Sunday morning back. As Adriana and I walked on stage at the Theatre Royal, Windsor there were both cheers and tears from church members.

The plan was to let Adriana say a few words and then keep a low profile for several months to settle in. But something unexpected happened as we just stood together. It felt as though the presence of the Holy Spirit, which we had experienced just a week before in the spiritual furnace of MCI in Bogotá, was also now touching people in a new way in England.

Everyone was listening intently as Adriana addressed the church for the first time. In English she said, "Good morning, everyone. I am very happy to finally be in Windsor and to meet my new church family. It's very special for me. I have been looking forward to this moment. Thank you for your very special welcome and for all your messages, beautiful messages, special messages; it touched my heart. Now that I am here, I must learn more English. Please help me."

She concluded, "I love your pastor. He's an answer to my prayers. Please, King's Church International, pray for me, pray for my husband, I will continue prayers for you. Okay, thank you."

I gave her a hug and kiss as people applauded Adriana and welcomed her to the church family. Then I preached on the same theme that had spoken to so many people the previous Sunday in Colombia. At the end of the message, scores of people came forward for prayer from each of the three levels of the theatre. Though it wasn't on the scale of what we had witnessed the week before in Bogotá, it carried the same spirit and DNA.

Our first months in England were interspersed with various overseas trips. A few weeks later, after our return from Bogotá, we were invited to tell our story and to minister to around 20,000 people at the G12 conference in the Philippines. Neither of us had been there before and we were instantly impressed by the warmth of the people and the "buzz" of the place. Of course, it helped that people so far from home spoke English; at least it was helpful for me.

Our hosts, Bishop Oriel Ballano and his wife Pastor Geraldine, treated us both as honeymooners as well as guest speakers. For a few days, they thoughtfully left us alone at a beautiful beachside resort by the South China Sea. When we returned to Manila where the conference was being held, we were provided with an elegant room in a place called "the city of dreams."

The host church had grown from 200 to 20,000 people in just ten years and the average age of their church members was 24. These young people flocked in great numbers to the conference, which was full of life and energy, that was more reminiscent of a pop concert than a traditional church service. After we had told our story, the people responded to the message in numbers that were even greater than what we had witnessed in Bogotá. For us, it was humbling and moving to see how our own journey of restoration and love was touching the lives of countless people in different cultures… a story that continued to unfold.

Just to make sure we really were married, we had five weddings in all. Technically, one wedding and four celebrations. In addition to Miami and Cali, we had two special wedding events on successive Sundays in Windsor, opposite the castle, with our home church, complete with speeches, prayers and videos of the first wedding. This time Adriana had yet another wedding dress. Thankfully, she didn't expect new rings.

Next, we headed to South Africa to introduce Adriana to King's Church International in Robertson. Everyone was keen to meet her and to hear what she had to say. Once again, she bravely stepped forward, speaking in her steadily-improving English, which she had honed by attending classes whenever she could and by constantly asking me to teach her.

As she spoke English more slowly and clearly than I did, most of the Afrikaners, who also spoke English as a second language, told us - in their typically forthright way - that they understood my star pupil's English better than my own. This became a great source of encouragement and amusement to Adriana.

After the Sunday services, our church family in Robertson generously arranged our fifth wedding celebration in one of South Africa's most stunning vineyards at Weltevrede, near Bonnievale outside of Robertson. Helpers from the church decorated an old cellar with fairy lights, candles, curtains, and flowers and prepared a great feast.

Adriana was ready for the occasion as we had bought a third, and final, beautiful white dress, and she had found a great hairdresser and makeup artist. She looked as beautiful as she had on our original wedding day six months before. My son, James, his wife Esther and their four children, Joseph, Joel, Eliana, and Joy, were there to greet us and follow us down the aisle. After worshipping the Lord and thanking God for His goodness, we were blessed by prayers and speeches from our South African friends and family.

By this time, we felt well and truly married after so many years of us both being single. In such a short space of time we had enjoyed a wedding and wedding celebrations on four different continents plus honeymoons in the Caribbean and by the South China Sea. And as if these were not enough indications of the Lord's goodness and mercy towards us, there was another romantic development on the horizon.

One year to the week from when the first sparks of

our relationship were ignited in Bogotá, Adriana and I were back in Colombia for another wedding.

Lina was glowing as she walked down the aisle side-by-side with her heroine and faithful Mum who happily presented her to Raul. And I had the privilege of preaching to the new couple. Pastor César led them their vows, with Wesley, James, Mel, and all the Colombian relatives, watching on. Now we truly were all one, big, international family.

Adriana and I could hardly take it all in. We had never known a year like it. What a momentous season of miraculous new beginnings and overflowing blessings it had been. We could not stop celebrating this complete resetting of our lives. For sure it was a "Year of Jubilee."

CHAPTER 14
LIVING HAPPILY EVER AFTER

"This is the start of something beautiful."[i] These lyrics, by singer Tim Halperin, certainly expressed what we felt when we got married. We believed then that ever increasing blessings awaited us, and we have not been disappointed.

Today, as we write this book, after eight years of marriage, we can now see even more clearly that, for all the wonderful developments in that first remarkable "Year of Jubilee," they were indeed just a foretaste of a new and beautiful future together.

So, are we truly still in love? Do we still delight in being together? Are we really living "happily ever after?" Adriana, "Si, si, and si." Wes, "Yes, yes and yes."

So much has happened in our time together that has brought us ever closer. Since we married…

- Adriana has learnt to fluently speak and preach in English.

- I still need to work a lot on my Spanish, but I know enough to generally understand what's going on… especially if Spanish speakers slow down.
- Adriana has joined me in becoming a British citizen and was in one of the last groups to pledge her allegiance to the late Queen Elizabeth II and her heirs.
- Adriana's two sons, daughter, son-in-law, and two granddaughters have moved from Colombia and now all live close to us in the UK.
- We have worked closely together as a couple leading the ministry of King's Church International in Windsor and Westminster, UK, and in Robertson, South Africa and speaking together at different conferences.
- We started a YouTube channel that has reached many thousands of people both inside and outside of church.
- We have safely negotiated the global pandemic…

All in all, we have shared many positive experiences together, but we also have had to learn to be there for each other in the tough times.

Our story could have so easily come to a sudden and tragic end on a notorious stretch of road outside of Cape Town, South Africa early one evening on 22 March 2018. I braked too hard on some uneven road and our hire car rolled over several times before coming to rest upside down. Fortunately, we weren't travelling too fast and this accident blackspot, normally filled with large trucks, had virtually no traffic at that moment.

As I came to my senses, I glanced over to check on my bride and was beyond relieved to see that, not only was she alive, but that she was also managing to scramble out of the car. I don't remember too much after that, but apparently the emergency services, thanks to Adriana, arrived quickly. What I can recall is an ambulance man telling me to keep my eyes open while he cut me free. I felt a great peace as I heard Adriana close by petitioning God for my life with great authority. At that moment, I was very thankful that I had married a wife who really knew how to pray.

After being rushed to hospital, we underwent several tests and x-rays. We were kept in hospital overnight for observation with nurses kindly arranging adjoining single beds for us to be able to hold hands and thank God together. Apart from some scratches, and in my case gashes, there was no lasting damage for either of us. After some days of rest following what one observer called "a miraculous escape," we were able to get on with our lives, grateful for the seatbelts that we were wearing and a Heavenly Father who had watched over us in our comings and goings.

This shared, near-death experience certainly focussed our minds on the fragility of life and bonded us even more than before. It made us even more determined to make the most of every day by being committed at a new level to developing the best possible marriage.

Both before and after the accident, we have faced

plenty of changes and challenges. Even when a marriage is made in heaven, it must be matured on earth. Ours has been no exception.

We have had to learn to show grace and mutual forgiveness to each other whenever there were misunderstandings and disagreements. Usually these were due to our considerable cultural and language differences, but sometimes it was simply because we are two imperfect individuals, still under God's construction, needing to adjust to being a couple after so many years of living as single people. Plus, to adapt the words of a famous book, Adriana is a woman from Venus via Colombia, and I am a British man from Mars.

Since we both increasingly value living in peace with one another and in unity with the Holy Spirit, we promised that, every single day, we would strive to maintain a zero-tolerance policy towards any form of hostility towards one another. Along the way we have managed to figure out some essential guidelines that have immensely helped our marriage to flourish.

1. Leave the old and embrace the new

In the Bible, Abraham and Sarah had to move out of the familiar surroundings of their home and family to enter the land that God had promised them. Ruth had to leave her old life and memories as a former wife and widow, to marry Boaz and to come into a new line of generational blessing.

The first disciples had to leave their fishing boats

behind to become, "fishers of men."[1] And Jesus Himself had to leave heaven to come to earth. Leaving old ways of life and re-ordering relationships with family and friends is also necessary when starting a new marriage. As Genesis 2:24 says, "A man leaves his father and mother and is united to his wife, and they become one flesh." At our stage of life, it was not so much leaving father and mother but rather prioritising our marriage over our much-loved children and grandchildren.

Adriana: *Obviously, my children are adults, but it was still a big emotional decision to leave them in Colombia. As a single mum, they were my closest relationships and I confided in them a lot. But when I married, I understood that my husband must now be my number one priority and that I must share everything with him. It was not right to expect him to fit in with my old way of life.*

Wes also has been sensitive not to make me adjust to his old way of life and ministry. We have both needed to make many changes. We have tried to create many good new stories for us and our families.

Wes: *To go forwards you can't be looking backwards even when you have had many good memories. Naturally, I love the deep-rooted relationships with my side of the family and their families, and I am happy with the development of great relationships with my new step-children and grandchildren. But Adriana is now my primary focus.*

Leaving the past, however, has also involved navigating all kinds of other changes that I hadn't expected, like finding more wardrobe space for Adriana and upgrading my own. I soon

---

1. Matthew 4:19

discovered that Adriana was on a mission to clear out many of my lovely old suits and familiar shirts.

Adriana could not believe the amount of stuff I still had from long gone eras and challenged me to prove how many of them still fitted me. Even though both of us laughed at my embarrassingly unsuccessful efforts to fit the past into the present, I still felt a pang when I had to say goodbye to several bags of ancient clothes.

2. Invest heavily to develop the best communication with each other

From the start we have had to work hard on our communication. It has involved long periods of studying together in the tropical heat of Cartagena, going to language classes in the sometimes-freezing UK, and constantly asking and answering questions about the meaning of words.

Despite the investment of time and effort, overcoming the language barrier was a much bigger challenge than we had imagined. At first, progress was slower than we wished. We both were disappointed that it took such effort to understand what we were trying to say to each other. Each of us longed to have a fluent conversation. Now that we can, we recognise that every moment of working at our communication was well worth it.

Effective communication, as we have discovered, is about far more than words. It's also about gentle tone, positive body language, encouraging smiles and reassuring touch. But words really do matter. Words have the power to build up or to tear down. Proverbs 18:21, says that "The tongue has the power of life and death, and those who love it will eat its fruit."

We have benefitted from developing two main areas of our communication by learning to…

Speak positively

Wes: *Adriana and I have been particularly careful with our language differences to choose words which are unmistakably affirming. Many times, we have had to use a translation app or thesaurus to find the most positive words for what we want to say. Even when there is an issue which needs to be discussed, we always try to 'speak the truth in love' aiming to build each other up.*

Adriana: *Every word we speak comes from our hearts. So, we must decide to guard our hearts and reject negative emotions, thoughts and comments. We should always seek to avoid judgemental words and declare words of faith. Always speak of the best possibilities and find something good to say.*

Listen carefully

Adriana: *Maybe this is true of many women, but certainly many Colombian women enjoy talking a lot. We like to express ourselves. After so many years of not having a husband, I love every opportunity that I have to talk with Wes, especially when we drink coffee together in the mornings or share a meal. But I have also found that I can bless Wes, as well as myself, when I stop talking and discover what he has to say. It says in James 1:19, "Everyone should be quick to listen, slow to speak." I have learnt so much by listening to Wes and of course I love it when he listens to me which he does… most of the time!*

Wes: *Truthfully, I love listening to Adriana. I am trying to* *develop my listening skills all the time because listening conveys value, and it greatly helps to know what someone, particularly your wife, is really thinking and feeling. And of course, I am relieved that Adriana is not like actress Sophia Vergara's feisty TV portrayal of a Colombian wife or the nagging woman from the book of Proverbs 27:15, who is like a "continual dripping on a rainy day." Instead, Adriana constantly rains words of encouragement on me.*

3. Be patient at all times

From the start of our relationship, we realised that we would need to be patient with each other because we were like babies learning to talk, even though we were both fluent in our own languages. And we have had to continue to stay patient in the face of many differences and adjustments.

The famous definition of love from 1 Corinthians 13:4-8, read at so many weddings including ours, has been particularly relevant for us. The sixteen characteristics of love that the apostle Paul outlines starts with patience and each of the following definitions of love are really descriptions of patience.

Patience, for example, is being kind to each other when another person doesn't do or say what you think or want. At the most basic level of a marriage, any couple needs to simply be kind and considerate to one another, to care for each other as best friends.

Patience, or love, is also not proud or egotistical. Patience means that you can't get frustrated with each other. Patience, as we first discovered on our honeymoon, means that we must always believe the best about each other.

The Message translation clearly expresses what we believe patience to be and is what we aspire to follow:

Love never gives up [love is patient]
   Love cares more for others than for self.
   Love doesn't want what it doesn't have.
   Love doesn't strut,
   Doesn't have a swelled head,
   Doesn't force itself on others,
   Isn't always "me first,"
   Doesn't fly off the handle,
   Doesn't keep score of the sins of others,
   Doesn't revel when others grovel,
   Takes pleasure in the flowering of truth,
   Puts up with anything,
   Trusts God always,
   Always looks for the best,
   Never looks back,
   But keeps going to the end.[2]

4. Operate as a team

Wes: *One of the first phrases I learnt in Spanish was "Dos son mejor que uno… two are better than one." We have found this to be so true in many ways.*

It's a quote from Ecclesiastes 4:9-12: "Two are better than

---

[2]. 1 Corinthians 13:3-7 MSG

one, because they have a good return for their labour: If either of them falls down, one can help the other up… Also, if two lie down together, they will keep warm. But how can one keep warm alone? Though one may be overpowered, two can defend themselves."

Adriana: *After so many years of having to do everything myself, it was a very big and special adjustment to be able to share everything in my life with someone who loves me and respects me. Being together has brought so much more strength and security to us as a couple. We have been able to achieve so much more at every level… in our family, in the church community and in our ministry.*

5. Keep the fires of romance burning

Romance of course involves sex. The Bible actually commands married couples in 1 Corinthians 7:5, "Do not deprive each other except by mutual consent." But romance is far more than sex as the Biblical Song of Songs makes clear. Romance is about mood, food, perfume, feelings, flowers, ambience, travel, all of which we have tried to factor into our marriage. Keeping the fires of romance going is as much the responsibility of the husband as it is of the wife.

Adriana: *Our engagement, wedding and honeymoon were all very romantic, but it did not stop there. Often after a long day and we come home to change, Wes will prepare a table of tapas with fairy lights, candles and background mood music. I love it. He often surprises me with flowers or a little present. He now chooses a lot of my clothes. He has a very good eye for what suits me. He will send me text messages of encourage-*

ment when I'm not expecting it. He always keeps me supplied with good coffee and makes sure we have time to enjoy it together no matter how busy our day is.

He regularly invites me out on dates and has driven me to visit most of the UK from the far north in Scotland to Land's End in Cornwall. Every year he has taken me away on our anniversary to places like Venice, Prague, and the Greek islands. In the year of Covid, when we couldn't travel, I made sure we had a very romantic environment in our house and garden. I never imagined that a British guy could be so romantic.

Wes: *For me, being romantic towards my wife is all part of being a good husband. I learnt a lot from my dad who came from a tough mining background but who always did his best to make my Mum feel special. And I have seen first-hand how well Pastor César treats his wife.*

Romance for me requires constantly deciding to keep paying attention to details and to always be thoughtful and generous. I never want to take Adriana for granted or for her to ever feel unappreciated.

Adriana certainly has also played her part to develop our romance. She is very encouraging of any romantic actions on my part and is multi-linguistic when it comes to communicating her love for me. She understands that we both like to be fluent in not one or two but all five love languages: words of affirmation, quality time, physical touch, acts of service, and receiving gifts.

Also, I think our romance has grown through a sixth love language: laughter. We have a similar sense of humour, and we can quickly see the funny side of many situations.

. . .

6. Always be thankful for one another

Adriana: *I am so thankful for a husband who thanks me for everything. I have never been thanked so much by anybody. He is thankful for every meal, maybe just because he is so relieved after Lina's first comments that I can cook after all! He's thankful for any jobs I do in the house and garden. He is thankful for all my time and effort in every area of church ministry. He is thankful that I pay attention to my make-up and clothes... I could go on.*

For me I am thankful above all for Wes's love and kindness. I am so thankful for his sincerity and integrity. I am thankful for his humility and generosity. I am thankful for all his dedication to God and for His commitment to helping people. I am thankful for the many ways he has helped me and looked after me so well. I am thankful that he values his wife so highly.

Wes: *Every day, without fail, I tell the Lord and Adriana how thankful I am that she is my wife. I always want her to know that I cannot count all the blessings that she has brought to my life. I am so grateful to her for all her love and her kindness. I am thankful for her thoughtfulness. I am thankful for her prayers and devotion to God. I am thankful for her partnership in the many areas of ministry. I am thankful for her faith and her friendship and for her sense of fun and Latina vibrancy. I am thankful for how she enriches my life in so many ways.*

7. Grow together in your love for God

Marriages flourish when there are shared foundational values and beliefs. From the start of our relationship, Adriana and I each wanted a marriage partner who really walked the walk of being a committed follower of Jesus. Even though we had many cultural and language differences, we were confident that whatever winds of change we would face, our marriage would be built on an unshakable rock of faith in Jesus Christ.

As a result, day by day and year by year we have prayed together, studied the Bible together, worshipped together, and ministered together. Our love for each other has grown exponentially and is directly linked to our love for God and our experience of His love for us. We believe that our marriage will continue to experience blessings of many kinds as we keep God at the centre. And that can also be true for your marriage, or for your future marriage.

I would like to encourage you, as I have encouraged many newly married couples over the years, to follow the advice of Mary to the servants at the wedding in Cana in Galilee to "do whatever"[3] Jesus says. For when they did, they opened the door to a miracle that they had never imagined. And, just as we have experienced, that miracle happened much later in the day than anyone had expected.

What had previously been just ordinary water ended up as very fine wine. In fact, there were huge stone jars filled to the brim. It was so good that when the master of ceremonies tasted it, he was amazed.

And then he said in words that well describes our Anglo/Hispanic love story: ***"You have saved the best till now."***[4]

---

3. John 2:5
4. John 2:10

FROM US TO YOU, WITH LOVE

When I first showed a photo of Adriana and myself to an old acquaintance, he carefully studied the image of my prospective bride. Then, for some moments, he quizzically looked up at me before refocusing his gaze on the beautiful Colombian lady in the picture. Finally, he said, "God must love you a lot my friend!"

I wasn't sure whether he was trying to build me up or put me down, but I immediately agreed with him. For I do believe that God loves me a lot, and I believe that God loves Adriana a lot. And both of us want to say to you that we believe that God also loves you a lot.

Our love story, with its many examples of unexpected favour, is part of a much bigger love story, the greatest love story ever told. It is the story of God's amazing love for the whole world. The most quoted verse in the Bible, which has been translated into 1,100 languages, could not be clearer, "For God *SO LOVED* the world that he gave his one and only Son, that whoever believes in him shall not perish but have eternal life."

This verse from John's gospel in chapter three and verse 16 tells us what everyone needs to know about God. He is not a vague impersonal cosmic force. He is not a God who is vindictive and nasty. Nor is He a God who is out to punish you, even though everyone has sinned against God. He is a God who is for you. He is a God who loves you so much that He gave His only beloved Son to die for you, so that you could live with forgiveness and freedom and be guaranteed a future of eternal life.

The Bible teaches that love is the very essence of God's character. "God is love," says 1 John 4:16. God's love is seen in Creation, in the faithfulness of His many promises in the Scriptures, in the teachings of Sermon on the Mount and in the life, ministry, death, and resurrection of Jesus Christ.

God's love is unmatched, unlimited, undeserved, and unconditional. It's for ALL the world.

God loves people of every race, ethnic group and religion… Jews, Muslims, Sikhs, Hindus, Buddhists, and those of no faith. He loves people of every tribe and language and people and nation. And as we've found, that includes Colombians and even the British!

Whatever a person's age, status, sex, or background, God reaches out in love not only to those who receive Him but also, incredibly, to those who reject Him and rebel against Him.

For sure, God is an awesome, Holy and Righteous God to whom everyone will one day have to give account, but His great love causes Him not to give up on unholy people. He hates sin, which is defined by what God's standards are not by what culture decides, but He loves sinners.

Jesus was known as a great friend of sinners. Jesus came to seek and to rescue all who are lost. John 3:17 says, "For God did not send his Son into the world to condemn the world, but to save the world through him." Or as Romans 5:8 puts it, "God demonstrates his own love for us in this: While we were still sinners, Christ died for us."

We do not get to know God's love because we are good and are deserving of His love but because God is good, and He extends His mercy towards us all. This is the amazing grace that we sang about in our wedding.

Adriana, despite having a traditional religious background, only discovered the reality of God's love for the first time at the age of 37, in a great outdoor service in Bogotá. And the whole story of her life changed from that moment.

In my case I have had the great privilege of experiencing this love since I was a child. And, for nearly all my life, I have had this great desire to share God's love far and wide. Every day I feel with a greater passion what my namesake, Charles Wesley, so well expressed in a famous hymn, *"O that the world would taste and see/the riches of his grace/the arms of love that compass me/would all mankind embrace."*[i]

The Prodigal Son, in the famous Biblical parable experienced this embrace. Even though He had left home and made a mess of his life, his Father, representing God the Father, had never given up on him. He was always looking out for him. One day, when his broken son came to his senses and humbly decided to return home, his dad spotted him while he was still a long way off. "… his father saw him and was filled with compassion for him; he ran to his son, threw his arms around him and kissed him," says Luke 15:21.

Maybe you have been living far from God for many years or maybe for a long time you have continued to faithfully follow God, even though things have been tough for you. In either case, Adriana and I pray that you will come closer to your Heavenly Father and receive His warm embrace.

His love will never fail you. He knows the story of your life and has kept watching out for you even in the most difficult or painful of experiences. He has heard, and He hears, your prayers.

You can trust that the same God who has guided us even when we were not always aware of it and who helped us when we least expected it, can also do the same for you. More blessings are in store for you than you can imagine. You too can be surprised by love.

A Prayer for New Beginnings

God hears and answers prayers. We have discovered this to be so true, and you can too. If you also want to see God's miracles in your life, we invite you to pray this prayer:

Heavenly Father,

Thank you for your great love when you sent your only Son, Jesus, to our world to pay the price for my sins and to draw me close to you.

Please forgive me and heal my heart. Give me the hope of new beginnings because of the resurrection of Jesus.

From today I turn from living my way to living Your way.

May I always know the comforting presence of the Holy Spirit as I follow you everyday and put my trust in You.

In Jesus' Name, Amen.

For sure, whenever you sincerely pray a prayer like this, you open the door to a whole new life. If you want any further information on how to grow as a Christian, we would love to hear from you and give you any help we can. Please contact us at www.kcionline.org or at surprisedbylove.co.uk

We pray that you will be blessed in every way.
Lots of love,
Wes and Adriana

ACKNOWLEDGMENTS

We are thankful for everyone who has helped us in the preparation of this book:

Jess Lamos and Natasha Airey for their sharp-eyed proof reading.

Nadia Bramley for co-ordinating permissions.

David Lee Martin for his timely and wise advice on publishing.

Raúl Arévalo for his preparation of the book for publishing and for the cover design.

Thanks also to Nicky and Pippa Gumbel, Dr RT Kendall, Barry and Batya Segal, and Adriana's long-time pastors, Johanna and Eliemerson Proença, for taking time out of their extremely busy lives to recommend this book.

Special thanks to everyone in our family who strongly supported us on our very unexpected journey of love.

Thanks to many fellow pastors, group leaders, church members, and other friends, both locally and globally, who have shown us kindness in so many ways. A special 'shout-out' to lifelong friends Terry and Margaret Beasley in the UK who have coordinated so many plans for us, and to Pastors William and Liliana Raad from

Miami who have so consistently opened their hearts and home to us.

Thanks again for the longtime support of Pastors Mike and Linda Peters from St. Louis and especially to Pastors César and Emma Claudia Castellanos. We very much appreciate their foreword to this book, and, above all, we are beyond grateful for their many faith-filled and wise words, personal example, prayers, and loving care which has been outstanding.

They are true shepherds revealing the heart of the greatest Shepherd of all who has guarded us and guided us through many mountains and valleys. We cannot thank God enough for His daily goodness and mercy. To God be all the glory.

LEGAL ACKNOWLEDGEMENTS

7. MEETING UP IN MIAMI

i. "Christ Arose" author Robert Lowry © Words: Public Domain; Music: Public Domain.

9. ENGAGED IN CARTAGENA

i. "Amazing Grace" author John Newton © Words: Public Domain; Music: Public Domain.

10. O HAPPY DAY

i. "This is Amazing Grace" (Farro/Riddle/Wickham) Copyright © 2012 WC Music Corp. / Phil Wickham Music (Admin. by BMG Rights Management [c/o Music Services, Inc.]) / Seems Like Music (Admin. by BMG Rights Management [c/o Music Services, Inc.]) / Sing My Songs (Admin. by BMG Rights Management [c/o Music Services, Inc.]) / Bethel Music Publishing (Admin. by Song Solutions www.songsolutions.org) All rights reserved. Used by permission.

ii. "Guardian" (Ben Cantelon/Stuart Garrard/Nick Herbert) Copyright © 2012 Thankyou Music (Adm. by Capitol CMG Publishing excl. UK & Europe, adm. by Integrity Music, part of the David C Cook family, songs@integritymusic.com)/ © So Essential Tunes (SESAC) / Stugio Music Publishing (SESAC) (admin at EssentialMusicPublishing.com). All rights reserved. Used by permission.

11. A VERY DIFFERENT KIND OF HONEYMOON

i. "Here is love, vast as the ocean" author William Rees; translator William Edwards © Words: Public Domain; Music: Public Domain.
ii. Ibid.

LEGAL ACKNOWLEDGEMENTS

14. LIVING HAPPILY EVER AFTER

i. "Something Beautiful" (Jordan Critz / Timothy Halperin) Used by kind permission of Third Orbit Publishing, Coffee And Chocolate, Endurance Bravo Music

FROM US TO YOU, WITH LOVE

i. "Jesus! the name high over all" author Charles Wesley © Words: Public Domain; Music: Public Domain.

ABOUT HOPE AND A FUTURE

Hope and a Future is the prequel to *Surprised by Love*. It tells the story of a family devastated by the loss of a beloved wife and mother to cancer. Yet, in their time of greatest sadness, they began to experience hope and profound healing as the children of Wes and Carol Richards - Wesley, James and Melody - met and fell in love with two sisters and a brother from the same South African family, resulting in three weddings and a new future.

"A compelling narrative of raw human emotion."

From the foreword by Jonathan Aitken, author and former British Cabinet minister

"The profoundly moving story of a family which has experienced both terrible tragedy and amazing blessing."

Nicky Gumbel, pioneer of the Alpha course

"Beautifully and brilliantly written, one of the most moving stories you are likely to come across."

R.T Kendall, author

For more information visit: hopeandafuture.org.uk

For more information

YOU CAN FOLLOW US ON SOCIAL MEDIA

Instagram: @wesrichards12 & @adrianarichards12

Or contact us at hello@wesrichards.co.uk or visit **wesrichards.co.uk**

———

KING'S CHURCH INTERNATIONAL:

King's Church International (KCI), is a non-denominational local church with a global vision, which was started in Slough in 1943.

KCI is a Bible based, multi-racial, and multi-generational church with people from more than 50 nations represented. Our offices and The King's House School, Windsor are in central Windsor with congregations meeting in the Thames Valley and Westminster, UK and in Robertson, South Africa.

KCI has strong links to one of the largest churches in

the world, MCI in Bogota, Colombia and its fast-growing network of churches around the world.

KCI is a registered charity which supports other charities, including a leading charity in Burkina Faso, one of the world's poorest countries, to which KCI has been a major and longstanding contributor.

To find out more please visit **kcionline.org** or email **hello@kcionline.org**

For more information and details of weekly podcasts, please visit:

Web: kcionline.org
   Instagram: @kingschurchinternational
   and @kci_london
   YouTube: King's Church International

Printed in Great Britain
by Amazon